NO LON
SEATTL

D0171868

LIC LIBRARY OF

Praise for *The Midnight Circus*

"Jane Yolen is, simply, a legend. The powerful fairy godmother of every writer working in mythic fantasy today. In these dark and wonderful stories, that legend proves itself true over and over again."
—Catherynne M. Valente, author of the Fairyland series

"Look this way, look that; blazing her consummate imagination against the shadows of human sorrow, Jane Yolen has done it again. *The Midnight Circus* delights."
—Gregory Maguire, author of *Wicked*

"Jane Yolen's stories are pure magic! They draw you in, beguile your senses, and paint the world in richer hues than you've ever seen. Her tales will haunt you in the very best way. I loved every word!"
—Sarah Beth Durst, author of *Race the Sands*

"Nebula Award winner Yolen follows *How to Fracture a Fairy Tale* with another, slightly more sinister collection of delightfully dark fairy tales. Each of the 16 stories is coupled with a companion poem and fascinating story notes that allow readers to delve into Yolen's magical worlds . . . Yolen's many fans will be thrilled."
—*Publishers Weekly*

"Some stories, like 'Inscription,' read like Celtic folktales while 'Requiem Antarctica' is a Jamesian tale of creeping madness at the ends of the Earth, and 'An Infestation of Angels' is a retelling of the book of Exodus. And if the stories themselves somehow aren't enough, each is accompanied by a poem that extends its themes into evocative verse. Haunting stories from a modern master."
—*Kirkus*

"*The Midnight Circus* sings with magic, darkness, and wonder—perfect for anyone who has ever loved a fairy tale. Thrilling and chilling all at once, this collection of stories will keep you riveted long after your bedtime, no matter your age."
—Meagan Spooner, author of the Starbound Trilogy

"5/5 stars. A wonderful collection of short stories! Each one is its own self-contained story that is just perfection."
—*Ash & Books*

Praise for the Jane Yolen Classic Fantasy collections

On 2018 World Fantasy Award Winner *The Emerald Circus*

★"These delightful retellings of favorite stories will captivate newcomers and fans of Yolen."
—*Library Journal*, starred review

★ "These highly entertaining retellings are perfect for teen fans of fairy tales and classic literature, though they are easily enjoyed without any background knowledge."
—*School Library Journal*, starred review

"Jane Yolen facets her glittering stories with the craft of a master jeweller. Everything she writes, including *The Emerald Circus*, is original and timeless."
—Elizabeth Wein, author of *Code Name Verity*

On 2019 Anne Izard Storytelling Award Winner *How to Fracture a Fairy Tale*

"This collection is Jane Yolen at her best."
—Patricia C. Wrede, author of the Enchanted Forest Chronicles

"Yolen takes well-known fairy tales and splits them apart, sometimes leaving them still quite familiar and other times shining a light from an unfamiliar angle to reveal new truths and possibilities."
—Margo Kelly, author of *Unlocked*

"A master storyteller at her best. I've been a fan of Jane Yolen and fractured fairytales for years and this collection doesn't disappoint."
—Chanda Hahn, bestselling author of *Reign*

Praise for Jane Yolen

"The Hans Christian Andersen of America."
—*Newsweek*

"The Aesop of the twentieth century."
—*The New York Times*

"Jane Yolen is a gem in the diadem of science fiction and fantasy."
—*Analog*

"One of the treasures of the science fiction community."
—Brandon Sanderson, author of *Mistborn*

"There is simply no better storyteller working in the fantasy field today. She's a national treasure."
—Terri Windling, author of *The Wood Wife*

The Hundredth Dove and Other Tales (1977)
Dream Weaver (1979)
Neptune Rising: Songs and Tales of the Undersea People (1982)
Tales of Wonder (1983)
The Whitethorn Wood and Other Magicks (1984)
Dragonfield and Other Stories (1985)
Favorite Folktales of the World (1986)
Merlin's Booke (1986)
The Faery Flag (1989)
Storyteller (1992)
Here There Be Dragons (1993)
Here There Be Unicorns (1994)
Here There Be Witches (1995)
Among Angels (with Nancy Willard, 1995)
Here There Be Angels (1996)
Here There Be Ghosts (1998)
Twelve Impossible Things Before Breakfast (1997)
Sister Emily's Lightship and Other Stories (2000)
Not One Damsel in Distress (2000)
Mightier Than the Sword (2003)
Once Upon a Time (She Said) (2005)
The Last Selchie Child (2012)
Grumbles from the Forest: Fairy-Tale Voices with a Twist (with Rebecca Kai Dotlich, 2013)
The Emerald Circus (2017)

How to Fracture a Fairy Tale (2018)

Graphic Novels
Foiled (2010)
The Last Dragon (2011)
Curses! Foiled Again (with Mike Cavallaro, 2013)

Stone Man Mysteries (with Adam Stemple)
Stone Cold (2016)
Sanctuary (2017)

THE MIDNIGHT CIRCUS
JANE YOLEN

THE MIDNIGHT CIRCUS

JANE YOLEN

TACHYON • SAN FRANCISCO

The Midnight Circus
Copyright © 2020 by Jane Yolen

This is a collected work of fiction. All events portrayed in this book are fictitious and any resemblance to real people or events is purely coincidental. All rights reserved including the right to reproduce this book or portions thereof in any form without the express permission of the author and the publisher.

Introduction: "Welcome to the Midnight Circus" copyright © 2020 by Theodora Goss

"Who Knew I Was a Writer of Dark Stories?" copyright © 2020 by Jane Yolen

"Afterword: From the Princess to the Queen" copyright © 2020 by Alethea Kontis

Interior and cover design by Elizabeth Story
Author photo © 2015 by Jason Stemple

Pages 240–242 constitute an extension of this copyright page

Tachyon Publications LLC
1459 18th Street #139
San Francisco, CA 94107
415.285.5615
www.tachyonpublications.com
tachyon@tachyonpublications.com

Series Editor: Jacob Weisman
Project Editor: James DeMaiolo

Print ISBN: 978-1-61696-340-8
Digital ISBN: 978-1-61696-341-5

Printed in the United States by Versa Press

First Edition: 2020
9 8 7 6 5 4 3 2 1

CONTENTS

Story Notes and Poems

WELCOME TO THE MIDNIGHT CIRCUS

Theodora Goss

In its three rings you will find a seal maiden and a queen of the sea, wolves that howl under the bed and wild girls who know how to fight for themselves, angels who are less than angelic, a boy who dreams of winter, a weaver of fates. . . . You may have seen some of the performers before (surely you've met Little Red Riding Hood?), but never quite like this. In this book, Jane Yolen weaves beauty and darkness, reality and the fantastic, imagination and the ordinary, as only she can.

I knew Jane from her stories long before I met her, so when I did finally meet her at a science fiction and fantasy convention where we were on the same panel, I was meeting *that* Jane Yolen. I was (don't tell her) a little intimidated, particularly because she knows more about fairy tales and fantasy than most professors in the field. She is formidably intelligent and articulate, unafraid to challenge viewpoints that are not historically sound or backed up by solid evidence. But she is also deeply kind and supportive to other writers, as she was and has been to me.

I first read her stories in the wonderful anthologies edited by Terri Windling and Ellen Datlow—the various fairy-tale anthologies beginning with *Snow White, Blood Red*, and, of course, *The Year's Best Fantasy and Horror* volumes, which were such an important part of my teenage years. Now I teach them in classes on fairy tales and the fantastic, along with her novel *Briar Rose*, which has the same beauty and darkness as the tales in this Midnight Circus. It is the story of a young woman who discovers that her grandmother's version of the Briar Rose fairy tale both hides and illuminates a dark secret. Like several of the stories in this volume, it is a tale of the Holocaust, told without any of the darkness diminished, but with the beauty of both the fantastical and of ordinary, everyday things. This is Jane's magical elixir, with three ingredients: the transformative beauty of fairy tale, which J. R. R. Tolkien called *faërie*; the sadness and cruelty of human life; and the strong, solid reality of our world. However fantastical her stories, they are grounded in bread and butter and wine, the landscape of Scotland or Massachusetts, the inescapable truths of history. This is why her stories always feel real and true—and wise.

The stories in this collection remind me of a garden of dark flowers: the old *rosa gallica* Cardinal de Richelieu, tulip Queen of the Night, hellebores and monkshoods and snake's head fritillaries, deep purple violets. They are darker than most of Jane's stories, but that darkness is there in much of her work, both fiction and poetry, because her writing is grounded in history and human nature, which have a dark edge. She has been called America's Hans Christian Andersen, and I can see why—Jane is as prolific and imaginative as the Danish writer of fairy tales. She has published so many books that you could read a new one every day for a year, and they are so different, in genre and subject matter and intended audience, that you would never feel as though she were repeating herself. She has also, by the way, won numerous awards, some of them multiple times, including the Nebula Award, Mythopoeic Fantasy Award, World Fantasy Award, Golden Kite Award, Rhysling Award . . . the list goes on. However, for me, a Jane Yolen story is fundamentally different from one of Andersen's tales in two ways. First, Jane is never sanctimonious. Her characters are sometimes good, sometimes bad, sometimes broken, but they are always treated as people, not vehicles for a message. And second, her stories contain a strong dose of her own common sense and pragmatism. They show us how we can survive in a difficult world and teach us what to value—in that sense, they are moral without being moralistic, wise guides to our lived reality. Andersen may sentimentalize, but she never does.

I have a personal list of favorite fantasy writers whom I read over and over again, because they capture what feels to me like true magic—both the numinous magic of fairyland and the ordinary magic of human life and love and hope. It includes such writers as Peter S. Beagle, Angela Carter, Susanna Clarke, John Crowley, Ursula K. Le Guin, Hope Mirrlees, Patricia McKillip, Sylvia

Townsend Warner, and T. H. White. And for a long time now, it has included Jane Yolen. She transports me to magical worlds and teaches me how to create magic myself through the ultimate spell, which is the one cast by a master storyteller. Her fiction and poems are a masterclass in craft. (Do, by the way, read the wonderful poems in the story notes. Jane is one of the rare fiction writers whose poetry is as rich and compelling as her prose.) I would recommend them to any aspiring writer, together with her wonderful book *Take Joy* on the pleasures and challenges of the writing life.

But you're not thinking about that right now, are you? No, you want the stories themselves, and I don't blame you. You want the mysterious Dog Boy, the man who worships owls, and the truth about Scott's Arctic expedition. Here you stand at the entrance to the tent, ticket in hand. You've come to see a performance.

You want marvels and delights, and I don't think you'll be disappointed.

Welcome to the Midnight Circus. Please take your seat. The show is about to begin.

WHO KNEW I WAS A WRITER OF DARK STORIES?

Jane Yolen

Actually, *I* didn't even know, though I'd had several darkish stories in the *Year's Best Horror Stories* collection, been nominated for horror awards, was in the Horror Writers of America for fifteen seconds or so, and read *Tales from the Crypt* comics as a young teen, huddled in the bathroom of our house, before creeping back to my bedroom with the (borrowed) comic safely down the front of my pants. And no, my parents never knew.

But while I have written the occasional vampire or werewolf story, three Holocaust novels, and a novella about the Russian Revolution with dragons, and books with ghosts and/or golems, witches (Baba Yaga appears in three different books—a novel in verse, a picture book for young kids, and a graphic novel), gargoyles, trolls, nasty fey princes, etc., I prefer my must-read dark matters to be somewhat limited. A frisson of terror rather than massive amounts of spilt blood. No pop-up all-devouring monsters, no bedwetting scares. No vicious and unrelenting tortures of women and children. No lusting after BRAINS!

Just plain old-fashioned M. R. James and that Other James—Henry, the author of *The Turn of the Screw*. Or more modern: *The Haunting of Hill House*, which is a 1959 gothic horror novel by American author Shirley Jackson. It was a finalist for the National Book Award, so that tells you something about the quality of the writing. It is still considered one of the best literary ghost stories of the 20th century.

And in a pinch I will reread the Mother of Gothics— Mary Shelley's *Frankenstein*. The Barry Moser illustrated edition.

So once Tachyon agreed they liked the idea of *Midnight Circus*, I began to research my collections, magazines, and journals to see whether I had enough stories to fill the book. I started with our database and then reread stories of mine in *Asimov's* and *F&SF*. Then I tackled the anthologies in my attic library. Must be well over a hundred such volumes, each with a story (or stories) of mine safely held within.

I made lists, annotated them. Sent what I considered my A and B stories to Tachyon to find out what volumes or magazines they already had and which stories we needed to copy here in my office. I must have started—after that early cull—with forty dark stories I still liked. Who knew?

Then I deleted any that had been in my first two Tachyon collections.

I had about twenty-five stories left to send to Tachyon. Publisher Jacob Weisman and my buddy Jim DeMaiolo wrestled with who loved which stories most. I think they disagreed on three. Small arguments ensued. No blood was spilt.

Next we talked about which stories went first, last. No fingernails were pulled. I had been an editor with my own line of books for Harcourt, had also produced or co-edited a bunch of anthologies, so I knew the drill. (Wait, no drills, no carving knives, no box cutters, no. . . .)

Finally I wrote this intro, did the backmatter about each story, and chose which poem of mine worked best with the individual story, some poems published, some new.

In the end, with only a bit of sweat, we produced the book. You are now judge and jury of it all.

There will be no executions.

Much too bloody.

Jane Yolen

THE WEAVER OF TOMORROW

Once, on the far side of yesterday, there lived a girl who wanted to know the future. She was not satisfied with knowing that the grass would come up each spring and that the sun would go down each night. The true knowledge she desired was each tick of tomorrow, each fall and each failure, each heartache and each pain, that would be the portion of every man. And because of this wish of hers, she was known as Vera, which is to say, *True*.

At first it was easy enough. She lived simply in a simple town, where little happened to change a day but a birth or a death that was always expected. And Vera awaited each event at the appointed bedside and, in this way, was always the first to know.

But as with many wishes of the heart, hers grew from a wish to a desire, from a desire to an obsession. And soon, knowing the simple futures of the simple people in that simple town was not enough for her.

"I wish to know what tomorrow holds for everyone," said Vera. "For every man and woman in our country. For every man and woman in our world."

"It is not good, this thing you wish," said her father.

But Vera did not listen. Instead she said, "I wish to know which king will fall and what the battle, which queen will die and what the cause. I want to know how many mothers will cry for babies lost and how many wives will weep for husbands slain."

And when she heard this, Vera's mother made the sign against the Evil One, for it was said in their simple town that the future was the Devil's dream.

But Vera only laughed and said loudly, "And for that, I want to know what the Evil One himself is doing with *his* tomorrow."

Since the Evil One himself could not have missed her speech, the people of the town visited the mayor and asked him to *send* Vera away.

The mayor took Vera and her mother and father, and they sought out the old man who lived in the mountain, who would answer one question a year. And they asked him what to do about Vera.

The old man who lived in the mountain, who ate the seeds that flowers dropped and the berries that God wrought, and who knew all about yesterdays and cared little about tomorrow, said, "She must be apprenticed to the Weaver."

"A weaver!" said the mayor and Vera's father and her

mother all at once. They thought surely that the old man who lived in the mountain had at last gone mad.

But the old man shook his head. "Not *a* weaver, but *the* Weaver, the Weaver of Tomorrow. She weaves with a golden thread and finishes each piece with a needle so fine that each minute of the unfolding day is woven into her work. They say that once every hundred years there is need for an apprentice, and it is just that many years since one has been found."

"Where does one find this Weaver?" asked the mayor.

"Ah, that I cannot say," said the old man who lived in the mountain, "for I have answered one question already." And he went back to his cave and rolled a stone across the entrance, a stone small enough to let the animals in but large enough to keep the townspeople out.

"Never mind," said Vera. "I would be apprenticed to this Weaver. And not even the Devil himself can keep me from finding her."

And so saying, she left the simple town with nothing but the clothes upon her back. She wandered until the hills got no higher but the valleys got deeper. She searched from one cold moon until the next. And at last, without warning, she came upon a cave where an old woman in black stood waiting.

"You took the Devil's own time coming," said the old woman.

"It was not his time at all," declared Vera.

"Oh, but it was," said the old woman, as she led the girl into the cave.

And what a wondrous place the cave was. On one wall

hung skeins of yarn of rainbow colors. On the other walls were tapestries of delicate design. In the center of the cave, where a single shaft of sunlight fell, was the loom of polished ebony, higher than a man and three times as broad, with a shuttle that flew like a captive blackbird through the golden threads of the warp.

For a year and a day, Vera stayed in the cave apprenticed to the Weaver. She learned which threads wove the future of kings and princes, and which of peasants and slaves. She was first to know in which kingdoms the sun would set and which kingdoms would be gone before the sun rose again. And though she was not yet allowed to weave, she watched the black loom where each minute of the day took shape, and learned how, once it had been woven, no power could change its course. Not an emperor, not a slave, not the Weaver herself. And she was taught to finish the work with a golden thread and a needle so fine that no one could tell where one day ended and the next began. And for a year she was happy.

But finally the day dawned when Vera was to start her second year with the Weaver. It began as usual. Vera rose and set the fire. Then she removed the tapestry of yesterday from the loom and brushed it outside until the golden threads mirrored the morning sun. She hung it on a silver hook that was by the entrance to the cave. Finally she returned to the loom, which waited mutely for the golden warp to be strung. And each thread that Vera pulled tight sang like the string of a harp. When she was through, Vera set the pot on the fire and woke the old woman to begin the weaving.

The old woman creaked and muttered as she stretched herself up. But Vera paid her no heed. Instead, she went to the Wall of Skeins and picked at random the colors to be woven. And each thread was a life.

"Slowly, slowly," the old Weaver had cautioned when Vera first learned to choose the threads. "At the end of each thread is the end of a heartbeat; the last of each color is the last of a world." But Vera could not learn to choose slowly, carefully. Instead she plucked and picked like a gay bird in the seed.

"And so it was with me," said the old Weaver with a sigh. "And so it was at first with me."

Now a year had passed, and the old woman kept her counsel to herself as Vera's fingers danced through the threads. Now she went creaking and muttering to the loom and began to weave. And now Vera turned her back to the growing cloth that told the future, and took the pot from the fire to make their meal. But as soon as that was done, she would hurry back to watch the growing work, for she never wearied of watching the minutes take shape on the ebony loom.

Only this day, as her back was turned, the old woman uttered a cry. It was like a sudden sharp pain. And the silence after it was like the release from pain altogether.

Vera was so startled she dropped the pot, and it spilled over and sizzled the fire out. She ran to the old woman who sat staring at the growing work. There, in the gold and shimmering tapestry, the Weaver had woven her own coming death.

There was the cave and there the dropped pot; and last the bed where, with the sun shining full on her face, the old woman would breathe no more.

"It has come," the old woman said to Vera, smoothing her black skirts over her knees. "The loom is yours." She stood up fresher and younger than Vera had ever seen her, and moved with a springy joy to the bed. Then she straightened the covers and lay down, her face turned toward the entrance of the cave. A shaft of light fell on her feet and began to move, as the sun moved, slowly toward her head.

"No," cried Vera at the smiling woman. "I want the loom. But not this way."

Gently, with folded hands, the old Weaver said, "Dear child, there is no other way."

"Then," said Vera slowly, knowing she lied, but lying nonetheless, "I do not want it."

"The time for choosing is past," said the old Weaver. "You chose and your hands have been chosen. It is woven. It is so."

"And in a hundred years?" asked Vera.

"You will be the Weaver, and some young girl will come, bright and eager, and you will know your time is near."

"No," said Vera.

"It is birth," said the old Weaver.

"No," said Vera.

"It is death," said the old weaver.

A single golden thread snapped suddenly on the loom.

Then the sun moved onto the Weaver's face and she died.

Vera sat staring at the old woman but did not stir. And though she sat for hour upon hour, and the day grew cold, the sun did not go down. Battles raged on and on, but no one won and no one lost, for nothing more had been woven.

At last, shivering with the cold, though the sun was still high, Vera went to the loom. She saw the old woman buried and herself at work, and so she hastened to the tasks.

And when the old woman lay under an unmarked stone in a forest full of unmarked stones, with only Vera to weep for her, Vera returned to the cave.

Inside, the loom gleamed black, like a giant ebony cage with golden bars as thin and fine as thread. And as Vera sat down to finish the weaving, her bones felt old and she welcomed the shaft of sun as it crept across her back. She welcomed each trip of the shuttle through the warp as it ticked off the hundred years to come. And at last Vera knew all she wanted to know about the future.

THE WHITE SEAL MAID

O n the North Sea shore there was a fisherman named
Merdock who lived all alone. He had neither wife
nor child nor wanted either one. At least that was what he
told the other men with whom he fished the haaf banks.

But truth was, Merdock was a lonely man, at ease only
with the wind and waves. And each evening, when he left
his companions, calling out "Fair wind!"—the 'sailor's
leave'—he knew they were going back to a warm hearth
and a full bed while he went home to none. Secretly he
longed for the same comfort.

One day it came to Merdock as if in a dream that he
should leave off fishing that day and go down to the sea-
ledge and hunt the seal. He had never done such a thing
before, thinking it close to murder, for the seal had human
eyes and cried with a baby's voice.

Yet though he had never done such a thing, there was
such a longing within him that Merdock could not say no

to it. And that longing was like a high, sweet singing, a calling. He could not rid his mind of it. So he went.

Down by a gray rock he sat, a long sharpened stick by his side. He kept his eyes fixed out on the sea, where the white birds sat on the waves like foam.

He waited through sunrise and sunset and through the long, cold night, the singing in his head. Then, when the wind went down a bit, he saw a white seal far out in the sea, coming toward him, the moon riding on its shoulder.

Merdock could scarcely breathe as he watched the seal, so shining and white was its head. It swam swiftly to the sea-ledge, and then with one quick push it was on land.

Merdock rose then in silence, the stick in his hand. He would have thrown it, too. But the white seal gave a sudden shudder and its skin sloughed off. It was a maiden cast in moonlight, with the tide about her feet.

She stepped high out of her skin, and her hair fell sleek and white about her shoulders and hid her breasts.

Merdock fell to his knees behind the rock and would have hidden his eyes, but her cold white beauty was too much for him. He could only stare. And if he made a noise then, she took no notice but turned her face to the sea and opened her arms up to the moon. Then she began to sway and call.

At first Merdock could not hear the words. Then he realized it was the very song he had heard in his head all that day:

Come to the edge,
Come down to the ledge

Where the water laps the shore.

Come to the strand,
Seals to the sand,
The watery time is o'er.

When the song was done, she began it again. It was as if the whole beach, the whole cove, the whole world were nothing but that one song.

And as she sang, the water began to fill up with seals. Black seals and gray seals and seals of every kind. They swam to the shore at her call and sloughed off their skins. They were as young as the white seal maid, but none so beautiful in Merdock's eyes: They swayed and turned at her singing, and joined their voices to hers. Faster and faster the seal maidens danced, in circles of twos and threes and fours. Only the white sea maid danced alone, in the center, surrounded by the castoff skins of her twirling sisters.

The moon remained high almost all the night, but at last it went down. At its setting, the sea maids stopped their singing, put on their skins again, one by one, went back into the sea again, one by one, and swam away. But the white seal maid did not go. She waited on the shore until the last of them was out of sight.

Then she turned to the watching man, as if she had always known he was there, hidden behind the gray rock. There was something strange, a kind of pleading, in her eyes.

Merdock read that pleading and thought he understood

it. He ran over to where she stood, grabbed up her seal-skin, and held it high overhead.

"Now you be mine," he said.

And she had to go with him, that was the way of it. For she was a selchie, one of the seal folk. And the old tales said it: the selchie maid without her skin was no more than a lass.

They were wed within the week, Merdock and the white seal maid, because he wanted it. So she nodded her head at the priest's bidding, though she said not a word.

And Merdock had no complaint of her, his "Sel" as he called her. No complaint except this: she would not go down to the sea. She would not go down by the shore where he had found her or down to the sand to see him in his boat, though often enough she would stare from the cottage door out past the cove's end where the inlet poured out into the great wide sea.

"Will you not walk down by the water's edge with me, Sel?" Merdock would ask each morning. "Or will you not come down to greet me when I return?"

She never answered him, either "Yea" or "Nay." Indeed, if he had not heard her singing that night on the ledge, he would have thought her mute. But she was a good wife, for all that, and did what he required. If she did not smile, she did not weep. She seemed, to Merdock, strangely content.

So Merdock hung the white sealskin up over the door where Sel could see it. He kept it there in case she should want to leave him, to don the skin and go. He could have hidden it or burned it, but he did not. He hoped the sight of it, so near and easy, would keep her with him, would tell her, as he could not, how much he loved her. For he found he did love her, his seal wife. It was that simple. He loved her and did not want her to go, but he would not keep her past her willing it, so he hung the skin up over the door.

And then their sons were born. One a year, born at the ebbing of the tide. And Sel sang to them, one by one, long, longing wordless songs that carried the sound of the sea. But to Merdock she said nothing.

Seven sons they were, strong and silent, one born each year. They were born to the sea, born to swim, born to let the tide lap them head and shoulder. And though they had the dark eyes of the seal, and though they had the seal's longing for the sea, they were men and had men's names: James, John, Michael, George, William, Rob, and Tom. They helped their father fish the cove and bring home his catch from the sea.

It was seven years and seven years and seven years again that the seal wife lived with him. The oldest of their sons was just coming to his twenty-first birthday, the youngest barely a man. It was on a gray day, the wind scarcely rising, that the boys all refused to go with Merdock when he called. They gave no reason but "Nay."

"Wife," Merdock called, his voice heavy and gray as the sky. "Wife, whose sons are these? How have you raised them that they say *nay* to their father when he calls?" It was ever his custom to talk to Sel as if she returned his words.

To his surprise, Sel turned to him and said, "Go. My sons be staying with me this day." It was the voice of the singer on the beach, musical and low. And the shock was so great that he went at once and did not look back.

He set his boat on the sea, the great boat that usually took several men to row it. He set it out himself and got it out into the cove, put the nets over, and did not respond when his sons called out to him as he went, "Father, fair wind!"

But after a bit the shock wore thin and he began to think about it. He became angry then, at his sons and at his wife, who had long plagued him with her silence. He pulled in the nets and pulled on the oars and started toward home. "I, too, can say *nay* to this sea," he said out loud as he rode the swells in.

The beach was cold and empty. Even the gulls were mute.

"I do not like this," Merdock said. "It smells of a storm."

He beached the boat and walked home. The sky gathered in around him. At the cottage he hesitated but a moment, then pulled savagely on the door. He waited for the warmth to greet him. But the house was as empty and cold as the beach.

Merdock went into the house and stared at the hearth, black and silent. Then, fear riding in his heart, he turned slowly and looked over the door.

The sealskin was gone.

"Sel!" he cried then as he ran from the house, and he named his sons in a great anguished cry as he ran. Down to the sea-ledge he went, calling their names like a prayer: "James, John, Michael, George, William, Rob, Tom!"

But they were gone.

The rocks were gray, as gray as the sky. At the water's edge was a pile of clothes that lay like discarded skins. Merdock stared out far across the cove and saw a seal herd swimming. Yet not a herd. A white seal and seven strong pups.

"Sel!" he cried again. "James, John, Michael, George, William, Rob, Tom!"

For a moment, the white seal turned her head, then she looked again to the open sea and barked out seven times. The wind carried the faint sounds back to the shore. Merdock heard, as if in a dream, the seven seal names she called. They seemed harsh and jangling to his ear.

Then the whole herd dove. When they came up again they were but eight dots strung along the horizon, lingering for a moment, then disappearing into the blue edge of sea.

Merdock recited the seven seal names to himself. And in that recitation was a song, a litany to the god of the seals. The names were no longer harsh, but right. And he remembered clearly again the moonlit night when the seals had danced upon the sand. Maidens all. Not a man or boy with them. And the white seal turning and choosing him, giving herself to him that he might give the seal people life.

His anger and sadness left him then. He turned once more to look at the sea and pictured his seven strong sons on their way.

He shouted their seal names to the wind. Then he added, under his breath, as if trying out a new tongue, "Fair wind, my sons. Fair wind."

THE SNATCHERS

You could say it all began in 1827 (though my part of it didn't start until 1963) because that was the year Tsar Nicholas I decided to draft Jews into the army. Before that, of course, only Russian peasants and undesirables had to face the awful twenty-five-year service.

But it was more than just service to the state the Jewish boys were called to do. For them, being in the army meant either starvation—for they would not eat non-kosher food—or conversion. No wonder their parents said *kaddish* for them when they were taken.

After Tsar Nicholas' edict, the army drafted sons of tax evaders and sons of Jews without passports. They picked up runaways and dissidents and cleaned the jails of Jews. Worst of all, they forced the *kahal,* the Jewish Community Council, to fill a quota of thirty boys for every one thousand Jews on the rolls—and those rolls contained the names of a lot of dead Jews as well as living. The Russian census takers were not very careful with their figures. It was the slaughter of the innocents all over again, and no messiah in sight.

The richest members of the community and the *kahal* got their own sons off, of course. Bribes were rampant, as were forgeries. Boys were reported on the census as much younger than they were, or they were given up for adoption to Jewish families without sons of their own, since single sons were never taken. And once in a while, a truly desperate mother would encourage her sons to mutilate themselves, for the army—like kosher butchers—did not accept damaged stock.

In my grandfather's village was a family known popularly as Eight-Toes because that is how many each of the five sons had. They'd cut off their little toes to escape the draft.

So many boys were trying in so many ways to avoid conscription that a new and awful profession arose amongst the Jews—the *khaper*. He was a kidnapper, a bounty hunter, a Jew against Jews.

My Aunt Vera used to sing an old song, but I didn't know what it meant until almost too late:

I had already washed and said the blessing
When the snatcher walked right in.
"Where are you going?" he asks me.
"To buy wheat, to buy corn."
"Oh no," he says, "you are on your way,
Trying to escape . . ."

One of my uncles remarked once that the family had come over to escape the *khapers* in the 1850s, and I thought he said "the coppers." For years I was sure the Yolens were but one step ahead of the police. Given my Uncle Louis' reputation as a bootlegger, why should anyone have wondered at my mistake? But I learned about the *khaper*—the real one—the year I was sixteen. And I understood, for the first time, why my family had left Ykaterinoslav without bothering to pack or say goodbye.

I was sixteen in the early sixties, living with my parents and two younger brothers in Westport, Connecticut. My father, a member of a lower-class family, had married rather late in life to a young and lovely Southern Jewish intellectual. He had become—by dint of hard work and much charm—part of the New York advertising fraternity. He had also rather successfully shaken off his Jewish identity: of all the Yolens of his generation, he was the only one without a hint of an accent. If he knew Yiddish, he had suppressed or forgotten it. My mother's family were active leftists, more interested in radicalism than religion. I was reminded we were Jews only when we went— infrequently—to a cousin's wedding or bar mitzvah.

I was undersized, over-bright, and prone to causes. My glasses hid the fact that I was more myopic about people than things. Recently I had fallen under the spell of a local pacifist guru who was protesting American involvement in Vietnam even before Americans were aware we *were* involved. While my friends were playing football and discussing baseball stats, I was standing in protest lines or standing silently in vigils in the middle of the bridge over the Saugatuck River. I even took to writing poems, full of angst and schoolboy passion. One ended:

Death you do not frighten me,
Only the unknown is frightening.

which the guru's group published in their mimeoed newsletter. It was my first by-line, which my father, a staunch Republican, refused to read.

It was while I was standing next to Bert Koop, the pacifist guru, basking in his praise of my poetry and wishing—not for the first time—that *he* was my father, that I noticed the man in black. We were used to onlookers, who usually shouted something at us, then walked away. But he was different. Wearing a long, ankle-length black coat and high boots with the pants pushed into the tops, he stood in the shadow of the town library's front door. He had an odd cap pulled down to his eyebrows that effectively hid his face, though I could tell he was staring at us. He didn't move for long minutes, and I thought he was watching the entire line of us. It was only much later that I understood he had been staring at me.

"FBI?" I whispered to Bert.

"CIA," he told me. "But remember—we have rights." He turned his face toward the man in black, as if defying him.

I did the same. And then, as bravado took over—sixteen is the high point of bravado even today—I slammed my fist against my chest, shouting across the noise of the traffic: "Doug Yolen. American. I have my rights."

At that, the man in black nodded at me, or at least he tucked his chin down, which totally obscured his face. I turned to gauge Bert's reaction. He was smiling proudly at me. When I looked back, the man in the doorway was gone.

The next time I saw him, I was at a basketball game, having been persuaded by Mary Lou Renzetti to go with her. I had had a crush on Mary Lou since second grade, so it didn't take much persuading. She thought of me as her little brother, though we were the same age, give or take a couple of months.

The man was on the other side of the gym, where the Southport crowd sat in dead quiet because their team was losing, and badly. I didn't see him until the second half. He was wearing the same black coat and cap, even though it must have been 100 degrees in the gym. This time, though, it was clear he was staring at me, which gave me the shivers, bravado notwithstanding. So I turned away to look at Mary Lou's profile, with its snub nose and freckles. Her mother was Irish and she took after that side.

Jack Patterson made an incredible basket then and we all leaped up to scream our approval. When I sat down again, I glanced at the Southport benches. The man in black was gone.

It went on like that for days. I would see him for a

minute and then look away. When I looked back he wasn't there. Sometimes it was clear where he had gone, for a nearby door would just be closing. Other times there was nowhere for him to have disappeared.

At first I found it uncomfortable, spooky. Then when nothing at all happened, I tried to make a joke of it.

"So—you see that guy over there, Mary Lou?" I asked. "The one with the black cap?" We were standing outside in the parking lot after school. I gestured over my shoulder at the running track, now covered with new-fallen snow. "He's been following me."

She put her hand on my arm, so I enlarged on the story, hoping she'd continue to hold on. "He's probably heard my dad is rich or something and wants to kidnap me. You think my dad will give him anything? I mean after the report card I brought home? He'll probably have to send my dad one of my fingers or something to prove he means . . ."

"Douggie, there's no one there."

I felt her hand on my arm, the fingers tight. I liked how they felt, and grinned at her. Slowly I turned my head, careful not to jiggle her hand loose. He wasn't there, of course. The snow on the running track was unbroken.

I thought about saying something to my father then. Or to my mother. But the more I rehearsed what I could say, the sillier it sounded. And though I had made a joke of it with Mary Lou, the truth is that the report card I'd brought home the week before hadn't really put me in my parents' good graces. It was "Douggie—you're too bright for this!" from my father. And a searching, soulful look from Mom. To make matters worse, the twins brought home all As. But then so had I at age thirteen.

So I shrugged the whole thing off as nerves. Or glands. Or needing new glasses. Or someone playing a bizarre joke. Or a hallucination. Only I had never joined the drinking crowd at school. Wine gave me headaches and I hated the taste of beer, especially when it repeated up my nose. Drugs had yet to hit high school—or at least to hit our crowd. They filtered in slowly over the next few years so that by the time the twins were seniors, Todd had experimented with everything in sight, and Tim joined an anti-drug crusade. But that's another story entirely.

Finally I spoke to Bert Koop about it and he was, predictably, sympathetic. And—as it turns out—totally wrong.

"Definitely CIA," he said. "They've been bugging my phone, too. Probably going to try and get to me through you."

"Well, if they think going to war is brave," I said. "I'll show them what *real* courage is. I won't say a word."

"Death . . . ," Bert quoted, "you do not frighten me."

"Right," I said, and really meant it. After all, I had never actually seen anyone dead. Jews don't believe in open caskets. So death *didn't* frighten me. But the man in black was beginning to.

It was about a week after I first saw him that the man in black turned up at our house. Not *in* the house, but *at it*, walking slowly down the road. Grounded on weekdays 'til my grades improved, I had been working on my homework curled up on the sofa in the living room. I was pretty involved in writing a term paper on *War and Peace*. Tolstoy had been a pacifist, too, and I was writing about the difference between a war in fiction and a war in real life, especially Vietnam. I don't know what made me look up at that moment, but I did. And through the picture window I saw him walking along Newtown Turnpike toward the Weston line.

I leaped off the sofa, scattering my notes and the AFSC pamphlets about war resistance all over the floor. Sticking my feet quickly into boots without lacing them, I ran out the door after him. By the time I got down the driveway and to the main road, I was shivering uncontrollably. It was late November and we'd already had two snowfalls; I hadn't taken a coat. But I walked way past the Hartleys' house, at least a quarter mile on up the road, right to the Weston line.

There was no sign of him.

That night I came down with a raging fever, missed a whole week of school, an interfaith peace vigil I had helped put together, the start of the big basketball tournament, and the due date for my Tolstoy paper. Evidently I had also spent one whole day—twenty-four solid hours—ranting and raving about the man in black. Enough so that both my mother *and* my father were worried. They had called the town cops, who questioned my friends, including Mary Lou. A police car made special rounds the entire week by our house. It seems my father really *did* have a lot of money, and there had been a kidnapping just six weeks earlier of an ad man's kid in Darien. No one was dismissing it as a prank.

But then they found the gang that had kidnapped the Darien kid, she identified them all, and the special patrols stopped. And once I was well again, I swore it had all been some kind of wild nightmare, a dream. After all, I had a healthy distrust of the police because of my association with Bert Koop. I think everyone was relieved.

Except—and this was the really funny thing—except my father. He made these long, secret phone calls to his brothers and sisters, and even to his Uncle Louis, who scarcely had an aggie left, much less the rest of his marbles. My father rarely spoke to his family; they were the embarrassing past he'd left behind. But since my night of raving, he insisted on calling them every night, talking to them in Yiddish. *Yiddish!* After that, he started going to work late and driving the twins and me to school before getting on the train to the city. Further, he established a check-in system for all of us. I was sixteen and embarrassed; sixteen is the high-water level of being embarrassed by one's parents.

It was two weeks before I saw the man in black again. By that time, with my grounding rescinded—not because my grades had gone up but because we all had other things to think about—and Mary Lou starting to pay a different kind of attention to me, I had all but forgotten the man in black. Or at least I had forgotten he scared me. I had walked the long block to Mary Lou's for a study date. Study on her part, date on mine, but I still got to hold her hand for about a quarter of an hour without her finding an excuse to remove it. Her parents kicked me out at ten.

The moon was that yellow-white of old bone. It made odd shadows on the snow. As I walked, my breath spun out before me like sugar candy; except for the noise of my exhalations, there wasn't a sound at all.

I was thinking about Mary Lou and the feel of her hand, warm and a bit moist in mine, and letting my feet get me home. Since I had gone around that block practically every day since second grade—the school bus stop was in front of Mary Lou's driveway—I didn't need to concentrate on where I was going. And suddenly, right at the bend of the road, where Newtown Turnpike met Mary Lou's road, a large shadow detached itself from one of the trees. He had made no sound but somehow I had heard something. I looked up and there he was. Something long and sharp glittered in his hand. He was humming a snatch of song and it came to me across the still air, tantalizingly familiar. I couldn't quite place it, though a tune ran through my mind: "You are on your way trying to escape . . ."

I turned and ran. How I ran! Back past Mary Lou's, past the Pattersons', past the new row of houses that just barely met the two-acre standards. I turned left and right and left again. It was dark—the moon having been hidden behind clouds—then light once more and still I ran. I had no breath and I ran; I had a stitch in my side and I ran; I stood for a moment by the side of the road vomiting and vomiting up something and then nothing and I ran.

I got home at three a.m. My mother lay fast asleep on the sofa, a box of Kleenex by her side, her eyes red with crying. She didn't rouse when I slipped in the door. I thought of waking her, of hugging her with gratitude that I was home and safe. But I was so exhausted, I went right to bed.

I took off my shoes and, still in my clothes, lay down. A shadow detached itself from my closet. Something long and sharp glittered in its hand. I tried to scream and couldn't, then saw it was my father and relaxed.

"Dad . . . ," I began.

"This . . . ," he said, as he always did when he was going to punish me, "is going to hurt me more than it does you."

He was wrong of course. On cold nights, especially winter nights, that missing toe aches more than anything.

But I have never seen the man in black again.

WILDING

Zena bounced down the brownstone steps two at a time, her face powdered a light green. It was the latest color and though she didn't think she looked particularly good in it, all the girls were wearing it. Her nails were striped the same hue. She had good nails.

"Zen!" her mother called out the window.

"Where are you going? Have you finished your homework?"

"Yes, Mom," Zena said without turning around. "I finished." *Well, almost*, she thought.

"And where are you—"

This time Zena turned. "Out!"

"Out where?"

Ever since Mom had separated from her third pairing, she had been overzealous in her questioning. *Where are you going? What are you doing? Who's going with you?* Zena hated all the questions, hated the old nicknames. *Zen. Princess. Little Bit.*

"Just out."

"Princess, just tell me where. So I won't have to worry."

"We're just going Wilding," Zena said, begrudging each syllable.

"I wish you wouldn't. That's the third time this month. It's not . . . not good. It's dangerous. There have been . . . deaths."

"That's 'gus, Mom. As in bo-gus. 'Ganda. As in propaganda. And you know it."

"It was on the news."

Zena made a face but didn't deign to answer. Everyone knew the news was not to be trusted.

"Don't forget your collar, then."

Zena pulled the collar out of her coat pocket and held it up above her head as she went down the last of the steps. She waggled it at the window. *That*, she thought, *should quiet Mom's nagging.* Not that she planned to wear the collar. Collars were for little kids out on their first Wildings. Or for tourist woggers. What did she need with one? She was already sixteen and, as the Pack's song went:

Sweet sixteen
Powdered green
Out in the park
Well after dark,
Wilding!

The torpedo train growled its way uptown and Zena

stood, legs wide apart, disdaining the hand grips. *Hangers are for tourist woggers,* she thought, watching as a pair of high-heeled out-of-towners clutched the overhead straps so tightly their hands turned white from blood loss.

The numbers flashed by—72, 85, 96. She bent her knees and straightened just in time for the torp to jar to a stop and disgorge its passengers. The woggers, hand-combing their dye jobs, got off, too. Zena refused to look at them but guessed they were going where she was going—to the Entrance.

Central Park's walls were now seventeen feet high and topped with electronic mesh. There were only two entrances, built when Wilding had become legal. The Westside Entrance was for going in. The Fifty-ninth Eastside was for going out.

As she came up the steps into the pearly evening light, Zena blinked. First Church was gleaming white and the incised letters on its facade were the only reminder of its religious past. The banners now hanging from its door proclaimed WILD WOOD CENTRAL, and the fluttering wolf and tiger flags, symbols of extinct mammals, gave a fair indication of the wind. Right now wind meant little to her, but once she was Wilding, she would know every nuance of it.

Zena sniffed the air. Good wind meant good tracking. If she went predator. She smiled in anticipation.

Behind her she could hear the tip-taps of wogger high heels. The woggers were giggling, a little scared. *Well,* Zena thought, *they should be a little scared. Wilding is a pure New York sport. No mushy woggers need apply.*

She stepped quickly up the marble stairs and entered the mammoth hall.

PRINT HERE, sang out the first display. Zena put her hand on the screen and it read her quickly. She knew she didn't have to worry. Her record was clear—no drugs, no drags. And her mom kept her creddies high enough. Not like some kids who got turned back everywhere, even off the torp trains. And the third time, a dark black line got printed across their palms. A month's worth of indelible ink. *Indelis* meant a month full of no: no vids, no torp trains, no boo-ti-ques for clothes. And no Wilding. *How*, Zena wondered, *could they stand it?*

Nick was waiting by the Wild Wood Central out-door. He was talking to Marnie and a good-looking dark-haired guy who Marnie was leaning against familiarly.

"Whizzard!" Nick called out when he saw Zena, and she almost blushed under the green powder. Just the one word, said with appreciation, but otherwise he didn't blink a lash. Zena liked that about Nick. There was something coolish, something even statue about him. And something dangerous, too, even outside the park, outside of Wilding. It was why they were seeing each other, though even after three months, Zena had never, would never, bring him home to meet her mother.

That dangerousness. Zena had it, too.

She went over and started to apologize for being late, saw the shuttered look in Nick's eyes, and changed her apology into an amusing story about her mom instead. She remembered Nick had once said, *Apologies are for woggers and kids.*

From her leaning position, Marnie introduced the dark-haired guy as Lazlo. He had dark eyes, too, the rims slightly yellow, which gave him a disquieting appearance. He grunted a hello.

Zena nodded. To do more would have been uncoolish.

"Like the mean green," Marnie said. "Looks coolish on you, foolish on me."

"Na-na," Zena answered, which was what she was supposed to answer. And, actually, she did think Marnie looked good in the green.

"Then let's go Wilding," Marnie said, putting on her collar.

Nick sniffed disdainfully, but he turned toward the door.

The four of them walked out through the tunnel, Marnie and Lazlo holding hands, even though Zena knew he was a just-met. She and Marnie knew everything about one another, had since preschool. Still, that was just like Marnie, overeager in everything.

Nick walked along in his low, slow, almost boneless way that made Zena want to sigh out loud, but she didn't. Soundless, she strode along by his side, their shoulders almost—but not quite—touching. The small bit of air between them crackled with a hot intensity.

As they passed through the first set of rays, a dull yellow light bathed their faces. Zena felt the first shudder go through her body but she worked to control it. In front of her, Lazlo's whole frame seemed to shake.

"Virg," Nick whispered to her, meaning it was Lazlo's first time out Wilding.

Zena was surprised. "True?" she asked.

"He's from O-Hi," Nick said. Then, almost as an afterthought, added, "My cousin."

"O-Hi?" Zena said, smothering both the surprise in her voice and the desire to giggle. Neither would have been coolish. She hadn't known Nick had any cousins, let alone from O-Hi—the boons, the breads of America. No one left O-Hi except as a tourist. And woggers just didn't look like Lazlo. Nick must have dressed him, must have lent him clothes, must have cut his hair in its fine duo-bop, one side long to the shoulder, one side shaved clean. Zena wondered if Marnie knew Lazlo was from O-Hi. Or if she cared. *Maybe*, Zena thought suddenly, *maybe I don't know Marnie as well as I thought I did.*

They passed the second set of rays; the light was blood red. She felt the beginnings of the change. It was not exactly unpleasant, either. *Something to do*, she remembered from the Wilding brochures she had read back when she was a kid, *with manipulating the basic DNA for a couple of hours.* She'd never really understood that sort of thing. She was suddenly reminded of the first time she'd come to Wild Wood Central, with a bunch of her girlfriends. Not coolish, of course, just giggly girls. None of them had stayed past dark and none had been greatly changed that time. Just a bit of hair, a bit of fang. Only Ginger had gotten a tail. But then she was the only one who'd hit puberty early; it ran in Ginger's family. Zena and her friends had all gone screaming through the park as fast as they could, and they'd all been wearing collars. Collars made the transition back to human easy, needing no effort on their parts, no will.

Zena reached into the pocket of her coat, fingering the leather collar there. She had plenty of will without it. *Plenty of won't, too!* she thought, feeling a bubble of amusement rise inside. *Will/won't. Will/won't.* The sound bumped about in her head.

When they passed the third rays, the deep green ones, which made her green face powder sparkle and spread in a mask, Zena laughed out loud. Green rays always seemed to tickle her. Her laugh was high, uncontrolled. Marnie was laughing as well, chittering almost. The green rays took her that way, too. But the boys both gave deep, dark grunts. Lazlo sounded just like Nick.

The brown rays caught them all in the middle of changing and—too late—Zena thought about the collar again. Marnie was wearing hers, and Lazlo his. When she turned to check on Nick, all she saw was a flash of yellow teeth and yellow eyes. For some reason, that so frightened her, she skittered collarless through the tunnel ahead of them all and was gone, Wilding.

The park was a dark, trembling, mysterious green: a pulsating, moist jungle where leaves large as platters reached out with their bitter, prickly auricles. Monkshood and stag bush, sticklewort and sumac stung Zena's legs as she ran twisting and turning along the pathways, heading toward the open meadow and the fading light, her new tail curled up over her back.

She thought she heard her name being called, but when

she turned her head to call back, the only sounds out of her mouth were the pipings and chitterlings of a beast. Still, the collar had been in her pocket, and the clothes, molded into monkey skin, remained close enough to her to lend her some human memories. Not as strong as if she had been collared, but strong enough.

She forced herself to stop running, forced herself back to a kind of calm. She could feel her human instincts fighting with her monkey memories. The monkey self—not predator but prey—screamed, *Hide! Run! Hide!* The human self reminded her that it was all a game, all in fun.

She trotted toward the meadow, safe in the knowledge that the creepier animals favored the moist, dark tunnel-like passages under the heavy canopy of leaves.

However, by the time she got to the meadow, scampering the last hundred yards on all fours, the daylight was nearly gone. It was, after all, past seven. Maybe even close to eight. It was difficult to tell time in the park.

There was one slim whitish tree at the edge of the meadow. *Birch*, her human self named it. She climbed it quickly, monkey fingers lending her speed and agility. Near the top, where the tree got bendy, she stopped to scan the meadow. It was aboil with creatures, some partly human, some purely beast. Occasionally one would leap high above the long grass, screeching. It was unclear from the sound whether it was a scream of fear or laughter.

And then she stopped thinking human thoughts at all, surrendering entirely to the Wilding. Smells assaulted her—the sharp tang of leaves, the mustier trunk smell, a sweet larva scent. Her long fingers tore at the bark, uncovering a scramble of beetles. She plucked them up, crammed them into her mouth, tasting the gingery snap of the shells.

A howl beneath the tree made her shiver. She stared down into a black mouth filled with yellow teeth.

"Hunger! Hunger!" howled the mouth.

She scrambled higher up into the tree, which began to shake dangerously and bend with her weight. Above. a pale, thin moon was rising. She reached one hand up, tried to pluck the moon as if it were a piece of fruit, using her tail for balance. When her fingers closed on nothing. she chittered unhappily. By her third attempt she was tired of the game and, seeing no danger lingering at the tree's base, climbed down.

The meadow grass was high, and tickled as she ran. Near her, others were scampering. but none reeked of predator and she moved rapidly alongside them, all heading in one direction—toward the smell of water.

The water was in a murky stream. Reaching it, she bent over and drank directly, lapping and sipping in equal measure. The water was cold and sour with urine. She spit it out and looked up. On the other side of the stream was a small copse of trees.

Trees! sang out her monkey mind.

However, she would not wade through the water. Finding a series of rocks, she jumped eagerly stone-to-stone-to-stone. When she got to the other side, she shook her hands and feet vigorously, then gave her tail a shake as well. She did not like the feel of the water. When she was dry enough, she headed for the trees.

At the foot of one tree was a body, human, but crumpled as if it were a pile of old clothes. Green face paint mixed with blood. She touched the leg, then the shoulder, and whimpered. A name came to her. *Marnie?* Then it faded. She touched the unfamiliar face. It was still warm, blood still flowing. Somewhere in the back part of her mind, the human part, she knew she should be doing something. But *what* seemed muddled and far away. She sat by the side of the body, shivering uncontrollably, will-less.

Suddenly there was a deep, low growl behind her and she leaped up, all unthinking, and headed toward the tree. Something caught her tail and pulled. She screamed, high, piercing. And then knifing through her mind, sharp and keen, was a human thought. *Flight.* She turned and kicked out at whatever had hold of her.

All she could see was a dark face with a wide hole for a mouth, and staring blue eyes. Then the creature was on top of her and all her kicking did not seem to be able to stop it at all.

The black face was so close she could smell its breath, hot and carnal. With one final human effort, she reached up to scratch the face and was startled because it did not feel at all like flesh. *Mask,* her human mind said, and then all her human senses flooded back. The park was suddenly less close, less alive. Sounds once so clear were muddied. Smells faded. But she knew what to do about her attacker. She ripped the mask from his face.

He blinked his blue eyes in surprise, his pale face splotchy with anger. For a moment he was stunned, watching her change beneath him, no longer a monkey, now a strong girl. A strong, screaming girl. She kicked again, straight up.

This time he was the one to scream.

It was all the screaming, not her kicking, that saved her. Suddenly there were a half-dozen men in camouflage around her. Men—not animals. She could scarcely understand where they'd come from. But they grabbed her attacker and carried him off. Only two of them stayed with her until the ambulance arrived.

"I don't get it," Zena said when at last she could sit up in the hospital bed. She ached everywhere, but she was alive.

"Without your collar," the man by her bedside said, "it's almost impossible to flash back to being human. You'd normally have had to wait out the entire five hours of Wilding. No shortcuts back."

"I know that," Zena said. It came out sharper than she meant, so she added, "I know you, too. You were one of my . . . rescuers."

He nodded. "You were lucky. Usually only the dead flash back that fast."

"So that's what happened to that . . ."

"Her name was Sandra Maharish."

"Oh,"

"She'd been foolish enough to leave off her collar, too. Only she hadn't the will you have, the will to flash and fight. It's what saved you."

Zena's mind went, *Will/won't. Will/won't.*

"What?" the man asked. Evidently she had said it aloud.

"Will," Zena whispered. "Only I didn't save me. You did."

"No, Zena, we could never have gotten to you in time if you hadn't screamed. Without the collar, Wild Wood Central can't track you. He counted on that."

"Track me?" Zena, unthinking, put a hand to her neck, found a bandage there.

"We try to keep a careful accounting of everything that goes on in the park," the man said. He looked, Zena thought, pretty coolish in his camouflage. Interesting looking, too, his face all planes and angles, with a wild, brushy orange mustache. Almost like one of those old pirates.

"Why?" she asked.

"Now that the city is safe everywhere else, people go Wilding just to feel that little shiver of fear. Just to get in touch with their primal selves."

"'Mime the prime,'" Zena said, remembering one of the old commercials.

"Exactly." He smiled. It was a very coolish smile. "And it's our job to make that fear safe. Control the chaos. Keep prime time clean."

"Then that guy . . ." Zena began, shuddering as she recalled the black mask, the hands around her neck.

"He'd actually killed three other girls, the Maharish girl being his latest. All girls without their collars who didn't have the human fight-back knowhow. He'd gotten in unchanged through one of the old tunnels that we should have had blocked. 'Those wild girls,' he called his victims. Thanks to you, we caught him."

"Are you a cop?" Zena wrinkled her nose a bit.

"Nope. I'm a Max," he said, giving her a long, slow wink.

"A Max?"

"We control the Wild Things!" When she looked blank, he said, "It's an old story." He handed her a card. "In case you want to know more."

Zena looked at the card. It was embellished with holograms, front and back, of extinct animals. His name, Carl Barkham, was emblazoned in red across the elephant.

Just then her mother came in. Barkham greeted her with a mock salute and left. He walked down the hall with a deliberate, rangy stride that made him look, Zena thought, a lot like a powerful animal. A lion. Or a tiger.

"Princess!" her mother cried. "I came as soon as I heard."

"I'm fine, Mom," Zena said, not even wincing at the old nickname.

Behind her were Marnie, Lazlo, and Nick. They stood silently by the bed. At last Nick whispered, "You okay?" Somehow he seemed small, young, boneless. He was glancing nervously at Zena, at her mother, then back again. It was very uncoolish.

"I'm fine," Zena said. "Just a little achy." If Barkham was a tiger, then Nick was just a cub. "But I realize now that going collarless was really dumb. I was plain lucky."

"Coolish," Nick said.

But it wasn't. The Max was coolish. Nick was just . . . just . . . foolish.

"I'm ready to go home, Mom," Zena said. "I've got a lot of homework."

"Homework?" The word fell out of Nick's slack mouth.

She smiled pityingly at him, put her feet over the side of the bed, and stood. "I've got a lot of studying to do if I want to become a Max."

"What's a Max?" all four of them asked at once.

"Someone who tames the Wild Things," she said. "It's an old story. Come on, Mom. I'm starving. Got anything still hot for dinner?"

REQUIEM
ANTARCTICA

with Robert J. Harris

In 1912 Robert Falcon Scott and four companions attempted to become the first men to reach the South Pole. Beaten to the Pole by the Norwegian Roald Amundsen, all of them perished on the return journey. It was eight months before their bodies were found huddled in a tent. The search party buried them there in the ice and the naval surgeon who examined them refused to divulge any medical details of the Polar party's end. It was a secret he carried with him to the grave.

I suppose a clergyman should be accustomed to keeping God's hours, but I could not help feeling vexed when the doorbell rang that chilly Saturday night. Most of my day had been taken up with a meeting of the deanery, and consequently my sermon for the following morning was still only half-written. If not for my determination to complete my task, I would have been abed some two hours. As it was, my brain was fogged with lack of sleep as I strove to explicate the mysteries of the Resurrection, seeking to do more than simply repeat what I had said the previous year. And—to be truthful—the year before that.

I was sitting in a half-dream when the door chime woke me, ringing like the tolling of a far-away bell. I shook myself out of an unsettling fancy about being summoned to watch spirits rising up from open graves. Pushing myself from my desk, I blinked in the lamplight, and then frowned down at my watch, which I had placed on the desk. Near eleven—and the text of the sermon not yet done.

The bell rang again, more insistently this time. I hurried from my study, barely restraining myself from shouting an irked warning to my visitor to show some patience.

I slid back the bolt and opened the door so abruptly that the woman who stood on the threshold took a timid step backward. At once I felt guilty for my own impatience and mustered what I hoped was a conciliatory smile.

In the gloom into which she had retreated she was well disguised, and it took me a few moments to recognize her. She was tightly wrapped in a thick green coat with a scarf bound over her head, for the weather outside was blustery with snow. Her pleasant, round face looked up at me diffidently. She had been at church sporadically over the past few years, but for the life of me I could not recall her name.

"I'm sorry to bother you at such an hour, vicar," she

apologized, "but Mr. Atkinson was quite frantic that I bring you."

"It's perfectly all right, I assure you." I wracked my brain for her name. "Perfectly all right." Now it was coming back to me. "God doesn't keep his eye on the clock, Mrs. Marchant," I added experimentally.

Her expression brightened only faintly but it was enough to confirm that I had recalled her name correctly. She was employed as a housekeeper by a Mr. Atkinson who had moved into Bay House about six years before but had never attended church. He was—I had been reliably told—a retired naval officer, and I had heard someone speak of him as having been something of an explorer in his youth. These days, by contrast, he was evidently so infirm that he was rarely sighted out of doors. I suppose I should have visited the old man before, offering him the consolation of prayer. But when he had first arrived in our village, I had sent over a welcoming letter. There had been no reply. I did not send another. I am not the proselytizing type. I believe that to force oneself on the unwilling only invites disaster. *In God's own time,* is my motto.

"Mr. Atkinson wishes to see me, you say?"

She nodded, her eyes wide. "He told me I had to come in person and fetch you. He was afraid you wouldn't respond to a phone call."

"Are you quite certain it cannot wait until morning? I have, er . . . business." I gestured vaguely toward the interior of the house. "It is very late." And in the morning I would be in church and unavailable, but I did not mention that. Just as I finished speaking, the clock in the hall began its toll.

"Mr. Atkinson is *unwell*," Mrs. Marchant said. There was no mistaking the genuine anxiety in her voice. The emphasis she laid on that last word implied more than the normal ill health of an invalid. I even detected a trace of a tear welling up in her eye. The natural conclusion was that Atkinson might be dead by morning.

I sighed in what I hoped was a good-natured manner, and signaled her in. Of course I would have to relent. The poor woman had just walked a good two miles in this inclement weather to find me.

"Just give me a moment to fetch my coat."

Relief spread across her face.

As I led her to the back of the parsonage where my car was parked, I had a flickering recollection of the bell in my recent reverie. That sense of being summoned for some extraordinary purpose returned to me with an irrational force that made my hand tremble as I tried to fit the key to the car door. But of course I did not speak of it. The devil is often in dreams. And in loose tongues as well.

Once we were seated and on our way, Mrs. Marchant appeared to relax. She even loosened her head scarf, the way another woman of another time might have loosened her stays. I looked back at the road.

"I assume Dr. Landsdale is in attendance?"

The housekeeper shook her head. I could see it from the corner of my eye. "Mr. Atkinson wouldn't allow me to call him," she said, staring off into the night.

"But if he is seriously ill . . . ?" I tried to keep any note of censure out of my voice.

"It was *you* he wanted, vicar, no one else," Mrs. March-ant insisted. She folded her arms about herself as though that gesture signaled an end to our conversation, like a full stop at the end of a sentence.

I decided not to press her. Clearly she was not minded to disobey her employer's instructions, however unreasonable they might seem. But I was determined to assess the situation upon our arrival and take whatever steps I felt necessary to aid the old man, even in the teeth of his own resistance.

Soon a wan yellow light from a pair of tall windows assured me that we were approaching Bay House. The handsome stone building, built around the turn of the century, was situated upon a small rise within sight of the sea whose low tide glimmered dully under the glow of a half moon. I pulled up by the front door, but Mrs. Marchant made no move until I climbed out and opened the passenger door for her. Even so, it was with obvious reluctance that she led me into the house.

In the well-lit vestibule, a ship's barometer upon the wall bore mute testimony to the unseasonable weather. To one side of a nearby doorway a stuffed gull stood upon a shelf, its wings outstretched, its beak agape as if in warning. On the opposite wall was a skillful watercolor painting of the sun rising over a snow-covered landscape.

Mrs. Marchant took my coat and hung it up, then pointed out the stairway.

"It's the first door facing you when you reach the top," she said. "The door's ajar. Just go right in. He's waiting for you. Can I bring you a cup of tea?"

"Not at the present, thank you." If I were to find myself attempting to argue Mr. Atkinson into accepting medical advice, it might be best for the housekeeper not to walk into the middle of a difficult scene. These old gentlemen can be devilishly reluctant. And the presence of a woman only makes them worse.

I ascended the stairway and, when I reached the open doorway, I could hear the labored breathing from within.

I stepped inside and saw Atkinson laid out in bed under a quilt, his head and shoulders propped up on three plump pillows. His hair was pure white, thick around the sides but with only a few wisps covering his crown. He was clean shaven—thanks, I assumed, to the attentions of Mrs. Marchant—and his features were of a lean, intelligent cast. One eye stared up brightly at me, the other seemed somehow dead, for it did not track as its mate did. What struck me most forcefully, however, was the air of melancholy that hung over him, even in repose. It was my immediate impression that this was not the result of his physical condition, but was a habitual facet of his character.

As I approached the bed, he fixed me with a stare that bespoke a fierce will.

"You are Reverend Kitson?" he asked. His voice, though tired, was that of a much younger man. In fact, as I got closer, I realized, he was not at all the aged seaman I had been led to expect but looked to be in his late forties, though hard living and rough seas, as well as the lingering illness, must have taken a great toll.

I also realized, somewhat latterly, that I had not donned my clerical collar before leaving the house.

"Yes, I am the vicar," I confirmed. "Mrs. Marchant brought me. I wrote you once."

He smiled, but it did not lift the melancholy that sat on his mouth. "I did not answer."

I shook my head, signifying that it did not matter. Not now.

His head shifted as though he were trying to nod in response, but was impeded by the pillows. "Mrs. Marchant is a good woman," he said, "and I will not let her go unrewarded."

I was surprised at the strength and clarity of his voice, which was very much at odds with his debilitated appearance. "I am certain that is not what . . ."

But his hand impatiently stopped my sentence. He had no time, that peremptory wave said, for the niceties of Christian dialogue. I was, I admit, glad of that. I have never been really good at this sort of thing. My parish work includes hospital visits, of course, but I do them with dread.

I moved closer and stretched out a hand that stopped short of touching his arm. "Do you not think we should phone for a doctor, Atkinson? You should really—"

He interrupted me this time with a savage cough that sent a brief flush to his pale young-old face. "I have had enough of his pills and injections," he rasped. "If death is coming, we should meet it with dignity, not cringing behind false comforts. All those potions do is to grant us a few hours of breath. I was a naval surgeon not so very long ago, and I know of what I speak."

I recovered my composure and said, "I knew you were a naval man, something of an explorer, I heard?" I did my best to sound conciliatory and accommodating. Numbing, even. His violent outburst had caused a visible deterioration in his state, and I did not want to provoke another.

He made no response to my inquiry, but raised a limp

arm to indicate a small cabinet by the wall. "Do you drink, Vicar?"

"I take a drop on occasion," I conceded, thinking on the hour. I had forgotten my watch, on the desk by my sermon, but surely it was closing in toward half eleven.

"Then have one now," Atkinson said. "There's a decent brandy in that cabinet that will warm you."

I hesitated, knowing there was still the sermon to complete when I got home again. But before I could decline politely he added, "You'll need a drink if you are to hear me through to the end."

There seemed no sense in upsetting him over so small a matter, so I accepted his offer. Then I pulled a chair up to his bedside and sipped from the modest measure I poured myself. In spite of the circumstances, I was pleasantly surprised to find that it was more than merely decent. I complimented him upon his taste, and this appeared to both amuse and calm him.

"Now that you are fortified against what is to come, we should get down to our business," he said, as if I were there for some sort of settling of a debt, "while there is still time."

"I assume you wish me to hear your confession." It would not be the first time I had heard the deathbed story of a man who had not seen the inside of a church since boyhood. Often what these fellows had to say was all the more poignant for the distance they felt yawning between themselves and their creator. I was good at this part of my vocation; listening was a skill I had been born with, unlike the writing of sermons, or parish small talk.

"It is only in part *my* confession," he responded with a

hint of irony. "It is another's confession that I must pass on to you, and I promise you will not thank me for it."

I was puzzled by his words, but I took another sip of the brandy and did not challenge him. It was only to be expected that his thoughts should become confused in this final extremity of his life.

"You are acquainted with the tragic consequences of Scott's Antarctic expedition?" he asked.

The question was unexpected, but I answered that, indeed, I was. "Who has not heard the tale of Captain Oates's noble sacrifice and the courageous end of Captain Scott and his men?"

"Yes, there have been several accounts published, but none—not even Scott's own journal—contains the truth," Atkinson said. "That truth has been a burden I have carried to this day. I am haunted by it. I have kept Scott's secret all these years, turning over and over in my mind whether I was doing the right thing by concealing it, or whether it would serve Scott and myself better for the world to know the truth. I have left it 'til too late to make a decision, so now I have no option but to pass that responsibility on to you. As a man of God, you of all people should know the value of discretion and be able to balance that against the stern demands of truth."

Indeed, I did not know if he had the right vicar for such an undertaking. God and truth, discretion and balance, were words in my vocabulary of service. But of late I would have been hard pressed to swear I knew what they meant. I was a bit old for a crisis of faith, but in fact it had thrust itself upon me. And the difficulty I was having writing my sermon was but one aspect of that thing. Still, it would not do to say so to Atkinson's face. The man was clearly dying. He needed my help. I did not need his.

So instead I nodded, setting aside the glass of brandy and leaning closer. "I am sure that you have made whatever decisions you thought best at the time. None of us make unflawed choices but any error can be excused if forgiveness is sincerely sought." That sounded as weak as one of my recent sermons, and I blamed it on the brandy. I vowed not to take another sip 'til the poor man was done.

"I seek nothing for myself," Atkinson insisted, "not even forgiveness. But this is my last opportunity to discharge a duty that was laid upon me all those years ago. Listen well, vicar—and try to understand."

He closed his eyes briefly—the one good one and the one that was dead—as though gathering his strength. Then his eyelids sprang open and he commenced his account, staring at the ceiling all the while. Someone more fanciful than I might have thought he beheld on that white plaster surface the harsh polar landscape that seemed to be haunting him, but not I. I merely waited for him to go on.

"I was not a member of Scott's first Antarctic expedition," he began, "not the one that left in 1900. But I was honored to be chosen as one of the crew of the *Terra Nova,* which set sail upon the second expedition in 1910. The aim of the earlier journey had been exploration and scientific study, but this second voyage, as we all knew, was a quest for the ultimate goal—the Pole itself." He stopped speaking for a minute, and licked his lips.

I gave him a glass of water that was sitting on the bedside table, holding it for him, while he drank two or three sips eagerly. He waited a moment before starting up again.

"Six months after setting sail from England, we landed at Cape Evans. By God, we were all awed by the imposing grandeur of the Great Ice Barrier and the distant mountains that guarded the hidden lands of Antarctica."

"Antarctica," I whispered. It was really a place to conjure.

"It was less than twenty years since man had first set foot upon that continent," Atkinson said, "and its frozen interior was as unexplored as the surface of the moon. In fact," and here he laughed without mirth, "without the benefit of radio, we were so isolated from the rest of the world, we might as well have been on the moon."

"I see your point," I muttered, though I did not entirely.

"The next several months were spent establishing our base and penetrating southward to lay down depots of food and fuel to supply the journey yet to come. It was during this time that we learned of the arrival of Amundsen and his Norwegians at the Bay of Whales. They had traveled south against all expectation with the avowed intention of being the first to reach the Pole."

As I suddenly recalled, they had. But I said nothing.

"There was no denying the sense of disappointment and resentment we all felt at Amundsen's intrusion, but we were not to be deterred. We were English, after all. Scott asserted vehemently that we still had every chance of beating our rivals in this race."

We were both silent for a moment, considering Scott's words, for hindsight is ever more accurate than foresight.

Then Atkinson continued. "You may not know this,

but Scott was subject to periods of gloomy abstraction. He was so resistant to any criticism of his plans, that any suggestions that ran counter to his expressed intentions were treated as little short of mutiny. I am a naval man, Reverend, so mutiny is not a term I use lightly.

"I was a member of the support party that accompanied Scott on the first leg of the journey, and I doubt if there was one of us who did not hope right up to the last he would be selected by Scott to join the summit party, those chosen few who would make the final push to the Pole.

"We crossed the frozen surface of the Great Ice Barrier and pushed on up the Beardmore Glacier to trek across the mainland of Antarctica itself. I can still hear the sound of the place, the immense stillness broken by an explosive crack—like a fusillade—as the ice responded to its own weight and pressure. There is nothing else quite like it in the world."

He began coughing again, and I offered him more water, but he waved it aside, impatient to be on with his tale.

"It was shortly before Christmas when we made our farewells to the summit party. Scott had chosen Oates, Wilson, Bowers, and Evans. I admit that I was both desolated and relieved at not being part of that group. A sense of foreboding hung over us all as we watched them disappear into the blank emptiness of the interior, but at the time we attributed it to our fear that it might already be too late to beat the Norwegians to our goal."

"As it was" I said.

"As it was," he conceded before continuing. "I returned

to Cape Evans where I took command of our base there. The daily routine kept us sane while we waited. But as the weeks went by, we became increasingly anxious about the fate of the summit party. Twice we probed as far south as we dared in the face of biting blizzards, but found no sign of them. Then the Antarctic night set in, and we could do nothing but wait through the long months of a ferocious winter."

Almost unconsciously I shivered, thinking of that place of cold comfort. Or perhaps it was that a midnight draught had come through the bedroom curtains, for the windows overlooked the bay and took the full brunt of the weather. But my tremor passed unnoticed by Atkinson, wrapped up as he was in his story.

"At last," he said, "the sun returned and conditions eased enough for us to set out on a proper search. It was now almost ten months since we had watched Scott and the others disappear into the frigid waste, and we held out no hope at all of their survival. Yet it was still a bitter blow when we sighted their tent drifted up with snow. I was not alone in my melancholy. I saw tears in the eyes of the others as we trudged toward that lonely shelter." His hands sketched the tent as he spoke.

"I ordered camp to be made a little way off while the tent was dug out. I was the first to enter. Of the five members of the Polar expedition only three had even made it this far. Two of them were fully wrapped in their sleeping bags, so that it was necessary to unfasten the bags to identify them. I could scarcely bear to look upon their frozen faces." His good eye closed again but this time the dead one kept staring up, as if gazing on the cold, wasted past.

"Do you wish to rest a moment?" I asked, worried that he had tired himself to no good end. But he once again waved an impatient hand.

"Let me finish," he said. "Let it *all* be finished." And then, as if my very interruption lent him strength, he returned to his tale.

"Dr. Wilson—whose artistic skills have left such striking images of the polar landscape—lay with his hands across his chest. He looked as though he had merely fallen asleep. Stocky little Bowers, his feet pointed to the door, also appeared to have passed away without pain. I checked them carefully, leaving Scott 'til the very last. But in truth I was months too late to offer them succor. This was a tomb, and we were the grave robbers. I was careful not to disturb the dead more than I had to, simply ascertaining the manner of their deaths.

"Between them lay our brave commander. He had thrown back the flaps of his sleeping bag and opened his coat, as if inviting the hostile elements to take him. His left hand was touching Wilson's arm, his right was across his own chest. Beneath the fingers of that hand, I saw an envelope. It was kept separate from the other letters that were laid out on a ground sheet nearby. The name inscribed on the envelope was my own."

"Ah," I said and, all unthinking, took a sip of the brandy. But my exhalation did nothing to stop the flow of Atkinson's story. He went on.

"Gently I pulled the envelope loose of the frozen body. Some indefinable instinct prompted me to conceal it in my pocket before I invited the others to enter—one by one—and bear witness to that tragic scene. We had been comrades to these dear, dead men. It was mere chance that they—and not we—had met eternity in this cold place. I left the others to their own thoughts, and retired to a spot well away from that awful tent, where I might open the envelope Scott had left for me and read the many pages he had written at the end without the others seeing me weep."

At this point Atkinson ceased his narrative and moved his hand stiffly to reach under the pillow behind him. He pulled out a fat envelope but had not the strength left to pass the thing on to me. I understood his intention and picked it up from the quilt where it had dropped from his enfeebled fingers. The envelope had yellowed, but the name *Edward Atkinson* could still be clearly discerned. The flap was open, but for some reason I hesitated to remove the contents.

"You *must* read it," Atkinson croaked, "otherwise you will have wasted your time—and mine also, which is considerably more precious, there being so much less of it." In spite of his bristling tone, he had clearly exhausted himself by relating his lengthy tale.

I pulled out Scott's letter and began to read it aloud, so Atkinson would know I was bowing to his will. Hearing my voice speaking what were obviously familiar words, he closed his eyes, but I do not think he slept.

My dear Atkinson, (the letter said)

Words cannot express my heaviness of heart over subjecting you to this extra burden when you have just found us in this sad condition. But I have no choice in the matter. Indeed the choice was made for me in London five years ago.

As the wind howls outside the tent, and the men lie dead by my side, I know the time has come for me to tell you all. I have long wrestled with this decision, wondering how great a disservice I do you. I even wondered for a while whether I was making my decision with a clear mind. The bleak desolation of Antarctica induces a singular state of consciousness quite different from that of ordinary life. One's priorities are shifted, attitudes are altered in a way that is imperceptible even to oneself, until one returns at last to the comforts and demands of civilization. I know this well, having lived through such shifts before. But you are a man of science. With your instruments you have laid open every secret cavity of the human corpus. If this is a disease—as I believe it to be—of the body and not the mind, who better to understand it than you?

Do I sound the mad man? Do not judge me yet, Atky. Read on, read on.

First I must tell you that while you may rightly grieve for the others, do not do so for me. Of them all, only I have attained the one goal that I truly sought: peace and a final freedom from the curse that has afflicted me for some five years now.

Yes—a curse. A disease *and* a curse. You must understand that or all is lost. If you have ever judged my behavior in this last expedition to have been difficult, even to the point of irrationality, I hope that these revelations will at least shed some light on my state of mind.

It was never my ambition to be an explorer, let alone one who charted the new lands of Antarctica. I was but a simple seaman. However, when Sir Clements Markham singled me out for that first expedition, I saw an opportunity to rise above the humble circumstances of an undistinguished naval career. The benefits proved even greater than I had anticipated. The burdens, greater still.

Returning to London after three years in Antarctica, I found myself to be a much sought-after celebrity. I now moved in an exotic milieu of writers, actors, and artists, not just hardened seamen. It quite turned my head, as much as a girl at her first ball. Indeed it was through my celebrity that I met my beautiful Kathleen. It is the one truly good thing I have done in this life. But do not, I pray you, burden Kathleen with what I am about to impart. Let her think me dead a hero. Only you will know otherwise. And—in this wild waste where I stay—I will know it as well.

Now to get to the meat of the matter. My cursed disease. It began in London, of that I am sure. Having led a conventional, perhaps even dull, life before—even as a seaman I'd not resorted to low pubs and lower women—I found it difficult to resist the allures of a more Bohemian existence, especially with my dear wife newly pregnant and unable to go out with me even to the more staid parties. Time after time, after she had retired early to bed, I would frequent areas of London I might once have shunned for fear of embarrassment or scandal.

What precisely occurred on the night that altered my fate so completely I have never been able to recall. Was it an infection I contracted from some whore? A mania passed on by tainted meat? Was I bitten by a mad dog? Raked by a rusty blade? Poisoned by some foreign tincture? Your surgeon's knife might have uncovered the seat of the infection. But five years on, discovering it would be like arguing First Causes with a Jesuit—fascinating but beside the point. Whatever it was that set me on this dark path is all lost in the miasma of those London rookeries. And confused by the great quantity of rum I had drunk with my low friends.

All I *do* know is that I found myself staggering down a deserted, muck-covered street in the early hours of the morning, my head pounding and my eyes curiously unfocused. I was also plagued by a peculiar thirst so intense that my throat was actually aching with it.

It was here that I was approached by a drunken vagrant begging for money. I tried to push my way past him, for he was a noxious, smelly brute, but he persisted in blocking my path.

"Guv'nor?" he said, his hand in my face.

It enraged me. *Enraged* me.

I do not speak here, Atkinson, of anger, or even a momentary spasm of annoyance, but of a pure, unreasoning rage.

Now as a very young man I had been known for my quick temper, but in later years I had mastered such outbursts. Now, however, I was possessed by a rage such as I had never before experienced. I trembled with it, like a tree in a fierce storm. Seizing hold of the raggedy man by the front of his filthy shirt I hauled him down onto the pavement with a speed and savagery he was powerless to resist. Before I could understand what was happening, I found myself with my teeth at his throat, sucking away his life's blood.

My horrible thirst quenched by this ghastly infusion, my head was finally cleared sufficiently for me to recoil in horror. The man lay under me, the side of his throat torn as if a wild beast had ravened there. Instinctively I wiped a hand across my mouth in an effort to erase the taste. My childhood squeamishness at the sight of blood briefly reasserted itself and, for a moment, I thought I was going to vomit right then and there.

I was sure I had killed the man and wondered what I was to do with the corpse. I knew no one would miss him. He was but a piece of filth. And there was no one else on the street to decry my deed. But to take him in my arms, to drag him to some smaller back alley—I did not know if I had the strength for it.

While I was thinking what to do, the man moaned piteously and I reeled back, more shocked than before. His eyelids began to flutter, like a girl at her first assignation. It appeared that he had merely swooned and was even now beginning to recover. I turned and ran from the scene as fast as my legs would carry me.

Upon my return home I cleaned myself up and made weak excuses for my evening's absence to dear, trusting Kathleen. It took all the composure I could muster to make it through that day, but by the end of it I was prepared to believe that what had occurred—however shocking—had been an isolated incident brought on by too much rum and base companionship, and that it would never repeat itself.

My shallow optimism was soon cruelly dashed. Within a day I felt once again the stirrings of that unnatural appetite and nothing I could do could stop me from feeding again.

Had I been a religious man I might have prayed for the curse to be lifted. I might have sheltered in a church and begged forgiveness from a priest. As it was, I had nothing but my own will with which to resist the dreadful craving. I put great store by my own powers. I should not have been so self-satisfied.

I succeeded for five days in resisting the thirst, much of those days spent in a state of isolation. I explained that I had a fever I did not wish to pass on to the other members of my household, especially to Kathleen in her delicate condition. Kathleen wanted to call a doctor, but I persuaded her that none was required.

I wrestled with my affliction, feeling it burn in my veins like hot mercury. My throat was parched beyond endurance and no amount of water or other liquid seemed to bring any relief. Brandy, port, tea, even sweet possets that cook sent up to me only made the thirst greater. I suffered alone, constantly pacing my room, and wearing out a pair of bedroom slippers in the five days of my torment.

I now believe that I might have cured myself had I been committed then to a cell. If I had allowed myself to be locked away before I took a second draught of that unnatural drink, the thirst—like a fever—might have burned itself out. But it was not to be. I relied on my will—and my will failed me.

When on the fifth evening I found myself standing over my dear Kathleen as she slept in her own room, my gaze lingering upon the vein that pulsed in her neck, my will at last broke. I rushed into the street, still in my dressing gown and second-best pair of slippers, and ran off into the night. I sought out once again those disreputable quarters of the city where I might pass unnoticed at that benighted hour, even dressed as I was.

I came upon a stray dog sniffing in the gutter and, in a vain hope, I grabbed hold of it and sank my teeth into its scrawny neck. With a choke of horror and distaste I flung the animal aside. Its blood was like bile, burning and bitter, but more bitter still was the revelation that only another human being could provide me with the sustenance I craved.

I staggered into a darkened alleyway, pale and trembling as the thirst racked my body. The sound of footsteps made me suddenly alert and—more like a wild animal than a man—I concealed myself in the shadows.

A London bobby passed by on his nocturnal beat. It was a mark of my desperate state of mind that the presence of the law did not frighten me in the least. I rushed upon him from behind and struck him down with one frenzied blow. He did not rise again.

Such was the extremity of my thirst by this time that it was all I could do to restrain myself from draining him utterly. I left him unconscious but alive and skulked off into the darkness, shamed by the bestial satisfaction I felt.

Although I had heard of men behaving as I did, it had only been in those horrific myths and legends and novels by hack writers who pandered to the basest tastes. And those stories were all vastly inconsistent with my own circumstances. I suffered no discomfort in the full light of day nor did I experience any of the other symptoms the popular imagination attributes to such a condition. My incisors did not grow long and pointed. My appetite for garlic was undiminished. I needed no home soil for comfort. There was only this awful, damnable thirst that only one horrid wine slaked.

Please understand, Atkinson, that I was entirely possessed by this cursed disease. Only when the thirst was satisfied, could I then act like any other man—eating and drinking and, to my shame, making love with the passion of a boy. But the thirst grew, and I had to satisfy it more often. Still, I took great care only to prey in the dark alleys and rookeries of London, where the unwashed and unwanted lived. I did not ever again drink from those folk whose lives were productive and regular. In this way, for a while, I excused myself as some sort of Grim Reaper, inflicting fear and pain only on those who deserved it. But in my saner moments I knew this to be untrue.

At last I understood that there was but a single course of action open to me if I was to preserve the honor of my family. So I filled a bathtub with hot water, and still in my dressing gown, climbed in. With two quick strokes of my shaving razor, I sliced open my veins at the wrists. The pain was but a moment, and then I slipped down under the water, the front of my gown rising and opening like the petals of a dark flower in the spreading red rain.

"Come death," I thought, and for the first time in months was at peace.

Nothing you have ever experienced can give you any inkling of the terror that possessed me when I awoke some time later, awash with my own blood, to find that I yet lived. I glanced down at my wrists, and saw that the wounds had healed themselves to such an extent that there was not even a visible scar.

I gripped the sides of the bath and clenched my teeth tight against the scream of anguish that tried to rip itself from my throat. But no sooner had my initial shock subsided than I became aware that the dread thirst was flaring up in me worse than I had ever felt it before, due—I had to believe—to the massive exsanguinations I had forced upon myself.

I hauled myself out of the bath, left the ruined gown on the floor, and hurriedly washed off all traces of the crimson which stained my body. Dressing with haste, I ran from the house leaving all goodness, morality, and will behind.

The rest of that night remains a blank to me, a merciful veil having been drawn across my memory by the bestial craving that had me in its grip. All I know is that by morning my thirst had been assuaged. I came home unseen, cleaned up the bathroom, and washed my own dressing gown. But for the curse itself there appeared no possibility of a cure. Even death—it seemed—would not have me.

What fate could I possibly subject myself to? It had

to be something so destructive as to render reanimation impossible. But there was nothing my disordered mind could think of. The prospect of recovering consciousness in some hideously dismembered state was even more terrifying and repugnant than the thought of continued life under the shadow of this affliction.

It was clear to me that until I could find a solution, I needed to devise some means whereby I could carry on my life without posing a threat to those whose good will meant so much to me. In a city such as London, there are women who will perform almost any service if adequately recompensed, and I had little trouble finding one suitable to my purpose. I shall call her Marie. Her real name does not matter in the slightest, and she was well paid for what I had her do. Better, in fact, than had I used her in the usual fashion.

Marie gave me the impression that—bizarre as my needs were—this was not the most repellent behavior she had been party to. Feeding sparingly, I learned that two or three visits with her per week were sufficient to prevent any uncontrollable outbursts of savagery on my part, at least in the beginning. Marie suffered no harm as a result of my . . . desires. And—to my even greater relief— she showed no sign of becoming contaminated with this dreadful infection herself. However, the shame of it all, the constant need for secrecy, and the knowledge of the irreparable harm it would do my family if the truth were ever exposed, all preyed horribly on my mind.

Consequently a brooding self-abhorrence came to dominate my waking hours. I found that I could no longer abide the sight of my own reflection in a mirror. Images of death struck me with a painful force that compelled me to avert my gaze from gazettes and books. Paintings in the museums—where Kathleen loved to walk with me—became abhorrent if they were about war or martyrdoms. And crowds—crowds were intolerable, for it was as though I could hear the very blood coursing richly through the veins as people pressed about me, upsetting the stability I strove so hard to achieve with my visits to Marie.

With each passing day it became more and more difficult to maintain a semblance of normal behavior. The birth of my son only exacerbated my gloom. His innocence threw into grotesque relief my own ever-present guilt.

I began to see that the only faint glimmer of hope I had was in mounting a second Antarctic Expedition. The aim of this journey was not merely to map and study, but to attain the greatest goal of all exploration—the South Pole itself. Perhaps there, amid the most intense cold to be found anywhere on earth, the heat of my unnatural thirst might be cooled.

I became obsessed with the grave site at Cape Adair where Hanson, the naturalist with the earlier Southern Cross party, had been buried. His was the only grave on that vast continent. I thought that I, too, might find the rest I longed for there at the frozen center of a bloodless land.

The task of raising finance for the expedition was both wearisome and frustrating, but I threw myself into it with a fierce energy and at last we were set to go. Kathleen already spoke of me as if I were a hero. I could not disabuse her of the notion. So I said nothing more.

We set sail on the *Terra Nova,* and while the others had their hopes set on the Pole, mine were set on peace. The close confines of the ship forced me into an unavoidable proximity with the other men, but fortunately the lowering temperatures did, indeed, temper my unnatural hunger. Tempered—but did not entirely destroy the thirst.

I was able to limit myself to only a fortnightly indulgence, using three different sources so as not to over-weaken anyone. I carried out my drinking during the hours of sleep, having by this time become well practiced at taking my guilty sustenance with a delicacy that left only the barest physical trace, and even this would fade in the course of a day. I never drank from the same man twice in a month. Any debilitating effects experienced by my comrades were thus attributed to the climatic conditions and our restricted diet.

Even you, my dear Atkinson, had my lips on your neck and never knew it. Your blood is a trifle sweet, more a Chianti than a cabernet.

The details of the trek to the Pole I have recorded in the diaries you will find in the green wallet under my bag. I have made every effort to be as truthful as possible while omitting those matters I am entrusting to you alone. I am sure you wondered why I decided to take an extra man on that last leg when we had originally planned for only four. By that time it had occurred to me that if the center of Antarctica were to prove my final resting place, then an extra man would be needed to haul the sleds on the return journey. I could not—of course—reveal my reasoning to anyone else, but here, now, you have it.

There was controversy about whether or not we should use dogs or men for the pulling, and I confess that my resistance to the use of dogs may have been colored by the incident I have already related to you, when I tried to drink from a beast rather than a man. Having dogs along made me terribly uncomfortable, to the point of nausea. And having along extra men for the work meant that I would need to visit individuals fewer times for my cursed drink.

My companions were the best of men, and I hoped that we might yet beat Amundsen in the race for the Pole, both for their sakes and for those we had left at home. For my own part, that goal had become second, for every step we took deeper into the vast, cold bleakness, the raging heat of my thirst cooled still further.

In the end, while I shared my crew's disappointment when we found the Norwegian flag and the note from Amundsen waiting for us, it was for me but a small distress. For there at the center of the stark icy world, I found myself without hunger or thirst or the raging blood that had plagued me for so long.

Here, I thought, *here is where I shall stay.*

I was already composing a letter to my dear Kathleen in my head. It was full of celebration and hope, even as it was a letter of farewell.

However, Amundsen's note drained the spirits from the men. Even seaman Evans, from whose simple good humor I had drawn such strength along the way, seemed drastically affected.

The men scarcely spoke to one another and took no joy

in the fact that they had made it that far, an accomplishment in itself.

I feared the mental oppression that was settling upon them might well spell their doom. The way back was to be made even more difficult with no sense of honor and reward at the end of the journey. Only the utmost determination can overcome the pitiless savagery of the Antarctic wastes, and the crew had lost that determination by coming in far second to the Pole.

I knew then that I would have to revise my plans. I could not—as I had so hoped—simply disappear into the vastness, sinking beneath the next fall of enveloping snow, my body frozen by the plunging temperatures of the Antarctic winter. I had to do all I could to lead these brave men to safety. Only then would I be free to make my way alone back into the icy embrace of the Antarctic. If I could turn them over to your good hands, Atkinson, I knew my work would be well done. Well done indeed.

But as you are reading this, you know all too well that the return journey proved even more of a trial than I had feared. The weather rapidly grew worse and we found our way blocked by yawning fissures and huge drifts.

Tragically it was Evans, that cheerful workhorse of our party, who was the first to succumb. The physical ravages of frostbite that assailed him were only the beginning. It soon became clear to us all that his mind had become affected. His fearful babblings did little good for the morale of the others. As we made our laborious way across the glacier on dwindling supplies, Evan's lucid periods became fewer and fewer, until he was at last incapable of proceeding.

To haul him on one of the sledges would slow us to such an extent that the party's fate would inevitably be sealed. I knew that it was up to me to end his suffering and give the others a fighting chance for survival.

So that night, while the party slept, their snores punctuating the sentence I had passed on young Evans, I crept over to him and lay down by his side. I put my gloved hands on either side of his face and gently turned it from me for I could not bear to watch him while I drank. He sighed once, like a child, as my teeth razored his neck but he did not otherwise wake. Silently I drank my fill.

As far as the others were aware, Evans had simply passed away from the effects of frostbite and the injuries he had sustained on the journey. But I could see in their faces that they could not help but be relieved that they were no longer faced with the awful choice of leaving him behind or dooming themselves by dragging him along. You must believe me, Atkinson, I did it for them, not for myself. The thirst was never the reason for his death, though I gained much strength thereby.

We were now four weeks out from the Pole and our progress had been depressingly slow. We pushed on and on against driving snow, our gear steadily more icy and difficult to manage. One by one we all became victims of the cruel cold and subject to bouts of snow-blindness.

While Wilson and Bowers did all they could to keep up the spirits of the party, Oates subsided into gloomy silence. His feet were swollen with frostbite and his old war wounds flared up under the hardship. Such was his agony that he was too enfeebled to help with pulling the sledges; it was all he could do to keep himself moving. In the tent he sat sullenly and stared at me. It was clear to him—as it was to the rest of us—that he was not going to make it much farther.

He drew me outside on the pretext of examining a damaged runner on one of the sledges, but we had no sooner shut the flap behind us than he took hold of my arm and yanked me well out of the hearing of Wilson and Bowers, who were still inside the shelter.

"I know what you think," he said in a voice that was as cold and thin as the wind whipping around us. "You think I'm done for and that I'm going to drag the rest of you down with me."

I tried to give him some reassurance, but he paid no heed to my words. His eyes burned with a feverish emotion and his voice rose in pitch.

"I saw what you did to Evans," he said. "I was not sleeping as you supposed. If not for the fact that the others have enough to contend with already, I would expose you for the foul creature you are."

I was so staggered both by this unexpected revelation and by the vehemence of his words that I was still gaping when he flung himself upon me and began to rain blows upon my head. For a man who had had trouble moving before, he was remarkably able.

"I will not go down so meekly!" he cried, and as he

continued his assault, he hurled all manner of abuse at me, which it would be fruitless and distasteful to repeat.

I had no option but to defend myself, striking back at him with all my might. The unthinking rage that had possessed me upon previous occasions rose up now, and I beat him viciously, pounding at him until there was no further resistance. By the time the red haze had faded from my eyes and I could think clearly again, he was dead.

I was panting from the exertion as I realized that I could not tell Wilson and Bowers the truth. Their morale was already at a low ebb. They would need every ounce of courage they could muster if I were to lead them back to safety.

I dragged Oates's body away, without even taking time to drink his blood, and buried him beneath the snow. Then, with my coat, I painstakingly brushed aside all signs of our struggle.

When I returned to the tent I told them that Oates—painfully aware of his condition and the fact that he was a burden on the rest of us—had followed a brave and honorable course. He had taken me aside to tell me what he planned to do, exacting a promise not to follow him. Then he had walked out into the icy waste to face his death in lonely dignity.

Neither Wilson nor Bowers questioned my tale, and indeed there was little reason for them to do so. Oates was a soldier, a proud man who had been wounded in battle, and it was entirely in keeping with his character that he would sacrifice himself for the good of his comrades. I promised Wilson and Bowers I would write of Oates's sacrifice in my journal, so that it would not be forgotten.

The words that I placed in his mouth were these: "I am just going outside and may be some time." You will agree, I am certain, that they have a noble ring.

We continued as best we could, hoping to reach the next depot before our already meager rations gave out. After only a few days, however, the most severe blizzard yet descended upon us, cutting off the wan sunlight and trapping us inside our tent. Even if we had had the strength to push on, we would have been hopelessly lost in the blinding storm.

It was obvious that the end was not far off. Wilson had long ago given up his diary and Bowers made only desultory meteorological notes, but now we commenced writing letters to the colleagues and the dear ones we would soon be leaving behind.

Once this task was done, my friends had nothing left to fortify their minds against the darkness that was coming upon us. Frostbite and cold kept them in constant discomfort. They wept at the thought of their families, and this so unmanned them that they were in mental agony as well.

I gave them the only gift I had left to give. While they slept fitfully, I granted them a quiet death by draining away their life's blood. In doing so I also gained for myself the sustenance I needed to see me through a few more days so that I could write this final testament.

Was it merely bad luck that stopped us here? Or is this place my destiny? I no longer believe in God, but I do believe that some awful Providence is clearly at work. I was not meant to return to even so remote an outpost of civilization as Cape Evans for—I am now sure—had I reached there, my bestial thirst would have erupted again. And in that place, so unlike London's dark rookeries, some dreadful incident would have exposed my awful secret. And then my dear Kathleen and my poor son would have borne the brunt of my dishonor.

Bury us all here together, Atkinson, and let us not be disturbed. Resist all attempts to bring us home. Say what you will—that this is a magnificent cathedral for our burial, or that it is fitting we stay here where we strove so hard against the elements. Only do not let others—even Kathleen—convince you to take our bodies back. As long as the ice has me in its grip, I am at peace. I have made my farewells in the other letters you see here, but I could not leave this tale untold. What you do with it is for you to decide, though I beg you to consider first and foremost my wife and son and their welfare.

Perhaps the truth should simply be allowed to die, but as the Antarctic wind howls outside, clawing at our little tent with its talons of ice, I pass this account on to you in defiance of mortality and the crushed hopes of a doomed expedition.

My last hope is that you will forgive me.

Yours ever sincerely,

R. Scott.

When I had finished reading the letter I saw that Atkinson was regarding me with an almost pitying stare.

"It is . . . incredible," I said, only too aware of the inadequacy of my words.

"When I read it the first time I thought so as well," Atkinson agreed. "I could only assume that Scott's mind had been unbalanced by the hardships of the journey and the deaths of his comrades. However, when I returned alone to his tent and examined the bodies of Wilson and Bowers, I found their condition to be entirely consistent with Scott's description of their end. They were drained of blood. And Scott's own body was what convinced me of the truth."

"What do you mean?"

"I could see now that his features were noticeably less disfigured by the eight months of winter than those of his companions. I took off my glove and touched my fingers to his frozen cheek. To my horror his eyes immediately began to move beneath the closed lids, as though he were experiencing a dream. His cracked lips parted, and he uttered two words in a dry whisper: 'Leave me!'

"I fled the tent and struggled to master myself lest any of my comrades suspect that something was amiss. The only conclusion I could draw was that the warmth of my touch, the blood beating beneath the pads of my fingertips, had been sufficient to rouse Scott momentarily from his frozen slumber."

I suppose my jaw dropped during the last of this recitation, though Atkinson was not done yet.

"I carried the watches and documents from the tent, removed the poles, and collapsed it. We built a cairn of stones over the graves and I read the burial service. We left for home, letting the Antarctic ice cover the grave and leaving Scott to the rest he so earnestly longed for."

As he finished his dreadful tale, Atkinson had become agitated. His face was reddening and there were tears in his weary eyes.

"But . . ." I said to Atkinson, "what you tell me is insane."

"I am a man of science, vicar," Atkinson said. "And I believe it. Can not you—a man of God—believe it, too?"

I shivered and looked away. For all that I spoke daily of God—and the devil—I still had great moments of doubt. But this strange confession somehow put all disbelief to rout. If this *thing* were true, then what else might be so? The miraculous birth, the even more miraculous Resurrection? I turned back, to thank the dying man for giving me back my faith, but he had one thing more to say.

"What haunts me most is this, Reverend," Atkinson said, and with some last miracle of strength, he sat bolt upright in the bed. "By his own testimony, Scott cannot truly die. He merely sleeps beneath the Antarctic ice, his thirst dormant. But what climatic changes might occur in millennia yet to come? In some distant age, the Polar ice melted, might he not rise again to haunt an unrecognizable world, to feed a thirst grown gigantic over a thousand frozen centuries?"

Atkinson's distress had now reached such a pitch that his body was shaken by violent convulsions. I seized him by the shoulders only to feel him slump into my arms.

"God will not allow that, my son," I said.

I settled him back down against the pillows and saw that the tranquility of death had overcome him at last. But my own newfound tranquility was forever shattered.

It had never occurred to me that there might be more than one kind of Resurrection. But what Atkinson, in his dying horror, had proposed was exactly that—a devil's resurrection. It was an unsettling, hideous, corrupting thought.

I would never, I supposed, finish that sermon now.

NIGHT WOLVES

When we moved into the old house on Brown's End, I knew the night wolves would move with us. And the bear. They had lived in every bedroom I'd ever had— the one in Allentown and the one in Phoenix and the one in Westport.

The wolves lived under my bed, the bear in my closet. They only came out at night.

I knew—I *absolutely* knew—that if I got out of bed in the middle of the night, I was a goner. You couldn't begin to imagine how big that bear was or how many teeth those wolves had. *You* couldn't imagine. But I could.

So I put the bear trap I had made out of Legos and paper clips in front of the closet. And I put the wolf trap I had built out of my brother Jensen's broken pocketknife and the old Christmas tree stand at the foot of my bed. And I kept the night-light on, even though I was ten when we moved to Brown's End.

That meant, of course, that no one dared come into my room in the dark, not Mom or Jensen, or even Dad, though we rarely saw him since he got married to Kate. And none of my friends stayed overnight.

It was safer that way.

Of course the minute it got to be light outside, the wolves and bear disappeared. I never did figure out where they went. And then I could go to the bathroom. Or get a new book from my bookcase. Or sit on the floor to put on my socks. Or anything.

Which meant winters were tough, especially now that we were living in the north, the dawn coming so late and all.

In Phoenix once, when I was eight, I was sick to my stomach and I just *had* to go to the bathroom. I waited and waited until it was almost too late, then made a dash over the foot of my bed. I managed to get out of the room in one big leap, my heart pounding so loud it sounded like I had a rock band inside. But I had to spend the rest of the night curled up in the tub because I could hear the wolves sniffing and snuffling around the bathroom door.

So when we moved to Brown's End without my dad, I expected the wolves and the bear. I just didn't expect the ghost.

I heard it on the very first night, a kind of low sobbing: *ooh-wooo-ooooooooo.*

The wolves heard it, too, and it made them nervous. They rushed around under my bed, growling and scratching all night, trying to get past the trap.

The next night the bear heard it, too. He thrashed

around so in the closet that when dawn came and I opened the closet door, my best sweater and my confirmation suit had fallen to the floor.

But the third night, the low sobbing turned into a cry that came from across the hall in the room where my mom slept. And then I was *really* scared.

"Mom!" I called out. I usually didn't like to do that for fear of reminding the wolves and bear that I was in the room with them. Then a little louder I called out, "Mom?"

She didn't wake up and call back that everything was all right.

So then I did something I *never* do. I called to Jensen, who was in the next room. Ever since Phoenix we'd had our own rooms. I hated to do that because he always teases me anyway, calling me a baby for needing a night-light. A baby! He was only eleven himself.

But Jensen didn't wake up, either. In fact I could hear him snoring. If I could only snore like that, I bet there wouldn't be any wolves or bear around my room.

I tried to sleep, but the ghost's sobbing came again.

I put the pillow over my head but somehow that made it worse.

I stayed that way until dawn. I didn't sleep much.

"Do you suppose this house is haunted?" I asked at breakfast, before we headed off to our new school.

Jensen snorted into his cereal. But Mom put her head to one side and considered me for a long while.

"Yeah, haunted," Jensen said. "By the ghosts of wolves. And a big ugly closet bear." I had made the mistake of telling the family about them when I was littler. And back when we were a family, Dad had teased me—and so had Jensen.

"Jensen . . . ," Mom warned.

So I didn't bring it up again. Not at breakfast and not at dinner, either. But when we went to bed that night, I borrowed two pieces of cotton from Mom's dresser and stuck them in my ears. Then I brushed my teeth, went to the bathroom, and jumped into bed. It was when I hit the bed the first time at night that the wolves knew it was time to wake up. And the bear.

Mom came in and kissed me good night. She turned on the night-light and turned off the overhead.

"Leave the door open," I reminded her. Not that she ever needed reminding.

And I lay down and quickly fell asleep.

It was well past midnight that I woke. The wolves and bear were quiet. It was the ghost sobbing loudly in Mom's room that woke me. I was surprised it hadn't wakened her. But then she didn't hear the wolves or bears, either. She said that since I did, I'm a hero every time I got into bed. I know I'm no hero—but I'd sure like to be.

The ghost went on and on and I began to wonder if it was dangerous. Bad enough that Dad was gone. If anything should happen to Mom . . .

I thought about that for a long time. After all, the foot of my bed was *even* closer to the door than it had been in Phoenix. And I was bigger.

I pulled the cotton out of my ears. The sound of the crying was so loud, the house seemed to shake with it. How could *anyone* sleep through that racket? I sat up in bed and the *wolves* began to growl. The bear pushed the closet door open and it squeaked a little in protest, inching out against the trap.

Ohowwwwwwwwwoooooooooo.

And then Mom's voice came, only terribly muffled. "Pete!" she cried. My name. And my Dad's.

Only Dad wasn't there.

That was when I knew that wolves and bear or no—I had to help her. I was her only hope.

"Get back, you suckers!" I shouted at the wolves, and threw the cotton balls down. They landed softly on the floor by the bed and muzzled the wolves.

"Leave me alone, you big *overgrown* rug!" I called to the bear, flinging my pillow at the closet door. The pillow thudded against the door, jamming it.

Without thinking it through any further than that, I jumped from the bed foot and landed, running, through the door. Two steps brought me into my mom's room.

That was when I saw it—the ghost, hovering over her bed. It was all in white, a slim female ghost in a long dress and a white veil. She was crying and crying.

"Why . . ." I said, my voice shaking, "why are you here? Who are you?"

The ghost turned toward me and slowly lifted her veil. I shivered, expecting to see maybe a shining skull with dark eye sockets or a monster with weeping sores or—I don't know—maybe even a wolf's head. But what I saw was like a faded familiar photograph. It took me a moment to understand. And then I knew—the ghost wore my mother's face, my mother's wedding dress. She was young and slim and . . . beautiful.

Behind me in my room, the wolves had set up an awful racket. The bear had joined in, snuffling and snorting. When I looked I could see red eyes glaring at me at the door's edge.

The ghost caught her breath and shivered.

"It's all right," I said. "They won't hurt us. Not here." I put my hand out to her. "And don't be sad. If you hadn't gotten married, where would I be? Or Jensen?"

The ghost looked at me for a long moment, considering, then lowered the veil.

"Pete? Honey?" My mom's voice came from the bed, sleepy yet full of wonder. "What are you doing in my room?"

"Being a hero, I guess," I said to her and to the wedding ghost and to myself. "You were having an awful bad dream."

"Not a bad dream, sweetie. A sad dream," she said. "And then I remembered I had you and your brother and it was all happy again. Do you want me to walk you back to your room?"

I looked over at the doorway. The red eyes were gone. "Nah," I said. "Who's afraid of a couple of night wolves and an old bear anyway? That's kid stuff." I kissed her on the cheek and watched as the ghost faded into the first rays of dawn. "I think I'm gonna like it here, Mom."

I marched back into my room and picked up the trap

from the foot of my bed, then the one from in front of the closet door. I heard whimpers, like a litter of puppies, coming from under the bed. I heard a big snore from the closet. I smiled. "I'm gonna like it here a lot."

THE HOUSE OF SEVEN ANGELS

My grandparents lived in the Ukraine in a village known as Ykaterinislav. It was a sleepy little Jewish town near Kiev, but if you go to look for it now, it is gone.

The people there were all hardworking farmers and tradesfolk, though there was at least one poor scholar who taught in the heder, a rabbi with the thinnest beard imaginable and eyes that leaked pink water whenever he spoke.

These were good people, you understand, but not exactly religious. That is, they went to shul and they did no work on the Sabbath and they fasted on Yom Kippur. But that was because their mothers and fathers had done so before them. Ykaterinislav was not a place that took to change. But the people there were no more tuned to God's note than any other small village. They were, you might say, tone-deaf to the cosmos.

Like most people.

And then one autumn day in 1897—about ten years before my grandparents even began to think about moving to America—a wandering rabbi came into the village. His name was Reb Jehudah and he was a very religious man. Some even said that he was the prophet Elijah, but that was later.

Reb Jehudah studied the Torah all day long and all night long. He put all the men in Ykaterinislav to shame. So they avoided him. My grandfather did, too, but he took out his books again, which had been stored away under the big double bed he and Grandma Manya shared. Took them out but never quite got around to reading them.

And then one of the village children, a boy named Moishe, peeked into Reb Jehudah's window. At first it was just curiosity. A boy, a window, what else could it have been? He saw the reb at dinner, his books before him. And he was being served, Moishe said, by seven angels.

Who could believe such a thing? Though the number, seven, was so specific. So the village elders asked the boy: How did he know they were angels?

"They had wings," Moishe said. "Four wings each. And they shone like brass."

"Who shone?" asked the elders. "The angels or the wings?"

"Yes," said Moishe, his eyes glowing.

Who could quarrel with a description like that?

Of course the village men went to visit Reb Jehudah to confirm what Moishe had seen. But they saw no angels, with or without wings. Like Balaam of the Bible, they had not the proper eyes.

But for a boy like Moishe to have been given such a vision . . . this was not the kind of rascal who made up stories. Indeed, Moishe was, if anything, a bit slow. Besides, such things had been known to happen, though never before in Ykaterinislav.

And so the elders went back to Butcher Kalman's house for tea, to discuss this. And perhaps Butcher Kalman put a bit of schnapps in their cups. Who can say? But they talked about it for hours—about the possibility of angels in Ykaterinislav, and in the autumn, too.

It was pilpul, of course, argument for argument's sake, even if they quoted Scripture. After a while, though, their old habits of nonbelief reclaimed them and they returned to their own work, but with renewed vigor. The crops, the shops, even the heder were the better for all the talk, so perhaps the angels were good for something after all.

Reb Jehudah knew nothing of this, of course. He continued his studying, day and night, night and day, wrestling with the great and small meanings of the law.

Now, one day an eighth angel came to visit him, an angel dressed in a long black robe that had pictures of eyes sewn into it, eyes that opened and closed at will. There was a ring of fire above the angel instead of a halo, and he carried an unsheathed sword. He held the sword above Reb Jehudah's head.

It was Samael, the Angel of Death.

Reb Jehudah did not notice this angel any more than

he had noticed the others, for he was much too busy poring over the books of the law.

The Angel of Death shuddered. He knew that as long as the rabbi was engaged in his studies, his life could not be taken.

All this Moishe saw, peeping through the window, for he had come every day to watch over Rabbi Jehudah instead of attending heder or working on his father's farm. As if he were another angel, though a bit grubby, with a smudge on one cheek and his fingernails not quite clean.

When Moishe saw the eighth angel, he shook all over with fear. He recognized Samael. He had heard about that sword with its bitter drop of poison at the tip. "The supreme poison," his teacher had called it.

"Reb Jehudah," Moishe called, "beware!"

The rabbi, intent on his studies, never heard the boy. But the Angel of Death did. He turned his awful head toward the window and smiled.

It was not a pleasant smile.

And before Moishe could duck or run, the Angel of Death was by his side.

"I will have one from this village today," said the angel. "If it cannot be the rabbi, then it shall be you." And he held his sword above Moishe's head.

Seized by terror, the child gasped, and his mouth opened wide to receive the poison drop.

At that very moment, the seven angels in Reb Jehudah's house set up a terrible wail; and this, at last, broke the good rabbi's concentration. He stood, stretched, and looked out of the window to the garden that he loved, it being as beautiful to him as the Garden of Eden. He saw a boy at his window gasping for breath. Without a thought more, the rabbi ran outside and put his arms around the boy to try and stop the convulsions.

Head up, the rabbi prayed, "O Lord of All Creation, may this child not die."

The minute the rabbi's mouth opened, the poison drop from the sword fell into it, and he died.

The Angel of Death flew away, his errand accomplished. He would not be back in Ykaterinislav until early spring, for a pogrom. But the seven angels flew out of the open Window, gathered up Reb Jehudah's soul, and carried it off to Heaven, where Metatron himself embraced the rabbi and called him blessed.

All this young Moishe saw, but he knew he could not tell anyone in Ykaterinislav. No one would believe him.

Instead he became a great storyteller, one of the greatest the world has ever known. His tales went around the earth, inspiring artists and musicians, settling children in their cots, and making the evenings when the tales were read aloud as sweet as nights in Paradise. "It was as if," one critic said of him, "his stories were carried on the wings of angels."

And perhaps they were.

GREAT GRAY

The cold spike of winter wind struck Donnal full in the face as he pedaled down River Road toward the marsh. He reveled in the cold just as he reveled in the ache of his hands in the wool gloves and the pull of muscle along the inside of his right thigh.

At the edge of the marsh, he got off the bike, tucking it against the sumac, and crossed the road to the big field. He was lucky this time. One of the Great Grays, the larger of the two, was perched on a tree. Donnal lifted the field glasses to his eyes and watched as the bird, undisturbed by his movement, regarded the field with its big yellow eyes.

Donnal didn't know a great deal about birds, but the newspapers had been full of the *invasion*, as it was called. Evidently Great Gray owls were Arctic birds that only every hundred years found their way in large numbers to towns as far south as Hatfield. He shivered, as if a Massachusetts town on the edge of the Berkshires was south. The red-back vole population in the north had crashed and the young Great Grays had fled their own hunger and the talons of the older birds. And here they were, daytime owls, fattening themselves on the mice and voles common even in winter in Hatfield.

Donnal smiled, and watched the bird as it took off, spreading its six-foot wings and sailing silently over the field. He knew there were other Great Grays in the Valley—two in Amherst, one in the Northampton Meadows, three reported in Holyoke, and some twenty others between Hatfield and Boston. But he felt that the two in Hatfield were his alone. So far no one else had discovered them. He had been biking out twice a day for over a week to watch them, a short three miles along the meandering road.

A vegetarian himself, even before he'd joined the Metallica commune in Turner's Falls, Donnal had developed an unnatural desire to watch animals feeding, as if that satisfied any of his dormant carnivorous instincts. He'd even owned a boa at one time, purchasing white mice for it at regular intervals. It was one of the reasons he'd been asked to leave the commune. The other, hardly worth mentioning, had more to do with a certain sexual ambivalence having to do with children. Donnal never thought about *those* things anymore. But watching the owls feeding made him aware of how much superior he was to the hunger of mere beasts.

"It makes me understand what is meant by a little lower

than the angels," he'd remarked to his massage teacher that morning, thinking about angels with great gray wings.

This time the owl suddenly plummeted down, pouncing on something which it carried in its talons as it flew back to the tree. Watching through the field glasses, Donnal saw it had a mouse. He shivered deliciously as the owl plucked at the mouse's neck, snapping the tiny spinal column. Even though he was much too far away to hear anything, Donnal fancied a tiny dying shriek and the satisfying snick as the beak crunched through bone. He held his breath in three great gasps as the owl swallowed the mouse whole. The last thing Donnal saw was the mouse's tail stuck for a moment out of the beak like a piece of gray velvet spaghetti.

Afterward, when the owl flew off, Donnal left the edge of the field and picked his way across the crisp snow to the tree. Just as he hoped, the pellet was on the ground by the roots.

Squatting, the back of his neck prickling with excitement, Donnal took off his gloves and picked up the pellet. For a minute he just held it in his right hand, wondering at how light and how dry the whole thing felt. Then he picked it apart. The mouse's skull was still intact, surrounded by bits of fur. Reaching into the pocket of his parka, Donnal brought out the silk scarf he'd bought a week ago at the Mercantile just for this purpose. The scarf was blood red with little flecks of dark blue. He wrapped the skull carefully in the silk and slipped the packet into his pocket, then turned a moment to survey the field again. Neither of the owls was in sight.

Patting the pocket thoughtfully, he drew his gloves back on and strode back toward his bike. The wind had risen and snow was beginning to fall. He let the wind push him along as he rode, almost effortlessly, back to the center of town.

Donnal had a room in a converted barn about a quarter of a mile south of the center. The room was an easy walk to his massage classes and only about an hour's bike ride into Northampton, even closer to the grocery store. His room was dark and low and had a damp, musty smell as if it still held the memory of cows and hay in its beams. Three other families shared the main part of the barn, ex-hippies like Donnal, but none of them from the commune. He had found the place by biking through each of the small Valley towns, their names like some sort of English poem: Hadley, Whately, Sunderland, Deerfield, Heath, Goshen, Rowe. Hatfield, on the flat, was outlined by the Connecticut River on its eastern flank. There had been acres of potatoes, their white flowers waving in the breeze. Earlier in the morning, he'd taken it as an omen and when he found that the center had everything he would need—a pizza parlor, a bank, a convenience store, and a video store—had made up his mind to stay. There was a notice about the room for rent tacked up in the convenience store. He went right over and was accepted at once.

Stashing his bike in one of the old stalls, Donnal went up the rickety backstairs to his room. He lined his boots up side by side by the door, he took the red scarf carefully out of his pocket. Cradling it in two hands, he walked over to the mantel, which he'd built from a long piece of wood he'd found in the back, sanding and polishing the wood by hand all summer long.

He bowed his head a moment, remembering the owl flying on its silent wings over the field, pouncing on the mouse, picking at the animal's neck until it died, then swallowing it whole. Then he smiled and unwrapped the skull.

He placed it on the mantel and stepped back, silently counting. There were seventeen little skulls there now. Twelve were mice, four were voles. One, he was sure, was a weasel's.

Lost in contemplation, he didn't hear the door open, the quick intake of breath. Only when he had finished his hundredth repetition of the mantra and turned did Donnal realize that little Jason was staring at the mantel.

"You . . ." Donnal began, the old rhythm of his heart spreading a heat down his back. "You are not supposed to come in without knocking, Jay. Without being . . ." He took a deep breath and willed the heat away. "Invited."

Jason nodded silently, his eyes still on the skulls.

"Did you hear me?" Donnal forced his voice to be soft but he couldn't help noticing that Jason's hair was as velvety as mouse skin. Donnal jammed his hands into his pockets. "Did you?"

Jason looked at him then, his dark eyes wide, vaguely unfocused. He nodded but did not speak. He never spoke.

"Go back to your apartment," Donnal said, walking the boy to the door. He motioned with his head, not daring to remove his hands from his pockets. "Now."

Jason disappeared through the door and Donnal shut it carefully with one shoulder, then leaned against it. After a moment, he drew his hands out of his pockets. They were trembling and moist.

He stared across the room at the skulls. They seemed to glow, but it was only a trick of the light, nothing more.

Donnal lay down on his futon and thought about nothing but the owls until he fell asleep. It was dinner time when he finally woke. As he ate he thought—and not for the first time—how hard winter was on vegetarians.

"But owls don't have that problem," he whispered aloud.

His teeth crunched through the celery with the same sort of *snick-snack* he thought he remembered hearing when the owl had bitten into the mouse's neck.

The next morning was one of those crisp, bright, clear winter mornings with the sun reflecting off the snowy fields with such an intensity that Donnal's eyes watered as he rode along River Road. By the water treatment building, he stopped and watched a cardinal flicking through the bare ligaments of sumac. His disability check was due and he guessed he might have a client or two as soon as he passed his exams at the Institute. He had good hands for massage and the extra money would come in handy. He giggled at the little joke: *hands . . . handy*. Extra money would mean he could buy the special tapes he'd been wanting. He'd use them for the accompaniment for massages and for his own meditations. Maybe even have cards made up: *Donnal McIvery, Licensed Massage Therapist*, the card would say. *Professional Massage. By Appointment Only.*

He was so busy thinking about the card, he didn't notice the car parked by the roadside until he was upon it. And it took him a minute before he realized there were three people—two men and a woman—standing on the other side of the car, staring at the far trees with binoculars.

Donnal felt hot then cold with anger. They were looking at *his* birds, *his* owls. He could see that both of the Great Grays were sitting in the eastern field, one on a dead tree down in the swampy area of the marsh and one in its favorite perch on a swamp maple. He controlled his anger and cleared his throat. Only the woman turned.

"Do you want a look?" she asked with a kind of quavering eagerness in her voice, starting to take the field glasses from around her neck.

Unable to answer, his anger still too strong, Donnal shook his head and, reaching into his pocket, took his own field glasses out. The red scarf came with it and fell to the ground. His cheeks flushed as red as the scarf as he bent to retrieve it. He knew there was no way the woman could guess what he used the scarf for, but still he felt she knew. He crumpled it tightly into a little ball and stuffed it back in his pocket. It was useless now, desecrated. He would have to use some of his disability check to buy another. He might have to miss a lesson because of it; because of *her*. Hatred for the woman flared up and it was all he could do to breathe deeply enough to force the feeling down, to calm himself. But his hands were shaking too much to raise the glasses to his eyes. When at last he could, the owls had flown, the people had gotten back into the car and driven away. Since the scarf was useless to him, he didn't even check for pellets, but got back on his bike and rode home.

Little Jason was playing outside when he got there and followed Donnal up to his room. He thought about warning the boy away again, but when he reached into his pocket and pulled out the scarf, having for the moment forgotten that the scarf's magic was lost to him, he was overcome with the red heat. He could feel great gray wings growing from his shoulders, bursting through his parka, sprouting quill, feather, vane. His mouth tasted blood. He heard the *snick-snack* of little neck bones being broken. Such a satisfying sound. When the heat abated, and his eyes cleared, he saw that the boy lay on the floor, the red scarf around his neck, pulled tight.

For a moment Donnal didn't understand. Why was Jason lying there; why was the scarf set into his neck in just that way? Then, when it came to him that his own strong hands had done it, he felt a strange satisfaction and he breathed as slowly as when he said his mantras. He laid the child out carefully on his bed and walked out of the room, closing the door behind.

He cashed the check at the local bank, then pedaled into Northampton. The Mercantile had several silk scarves, but only one red one. It was a dark red, like old blood. He bought it and folded it carefully into a little packet, then tucked it reverently into his pocket.

When he rode past the barn where he lived, he saw that there were several police cars parked in the driveway and so he didn't stop. Bending over the handlebars, he pushed with all his might, as if he could feel the stares of towns-folk.

The center was filled with cars, and two high school se-niors, down from Smith Academy to buy candy, watched as he flew past. The wind at his back urged him on as he pedaled past the Main Street houses, around the mean-dering turns, past the treatment plant and the old barns marked with the passage of high school graffiti.

He was not surprised to see two vans by the road-side, one with out-of-state plates; he knew why they were there. Leaning his bike against one of the vans, he headed toward the swamp, his feet making crisp tracks on the crusty snow.

There were about fifteen people standing in a semicircle around the dead tree. The largest of the Great Grays sat in the crotch of the tree, staring at the circle of watchers with its yellow eyes. Slowly its head turned from left to right, eyes blinked, then another quarter turn.

The people were silent, though every once in a while one would move forward and kneel before the great bird, then as silently move back to place.

Donnal was exultant. These were not birders with field glasses and cameras. These were worshipers. Just as he was. He reached into his pocket and drew out the kerchief. Then slowly, not even feeling the cold, he took off his boots and socks, his jacket and trousers, his underpants and shirt. No one noticed him but the owl, whose yellow eyes only blinked but showed no fear.

He spoke his mantra silently and stepped closer, the scarf between his hands, moving through the circle to the foot of the tree. There he knelt, spreading the cloth to catch the pellet when it fell and baring his neck to the Great Gray's slashing beak.

LITTLE RED

with Adam Stemple

Seven years of bad luck. That's what I think as I drag the piece of broken mirror over my forearm. Just to the right of a long blue vein, tracing the thin scars that came before.

There's no pain. That's all on the inside. It won't come no matter how much I bleed. No pain. But for a moment . . .

Relief.

For a moment.

Until Mr. L calls me again. "Hey, you, Little Red, come here."

Calls *me*. Not any of the other girls. Maybe it's because he likes my stubby red hair. Likes to twist his stubby old-man fingers in it. And I can't tell him no.

"You want to go back home?" he asks. "Back to your grandmother's? Back to the old sewing lady?" He's read my file. He knows what I will say.

"No. Even you are better than that." Then I don't say

anything else. I just go away for a bit in my mind and leave him my body.

The forest is dark but I know the way. I have been here before. There is a path soon, pebbly and worn. But my fingers and toes are like needles and pins. If I stay here, stray here too long, will I become one of them forever?

It's morning now, and I'm back, looking for something sharp. Orderlies have cleaned up the mirror; I think Mr. L found the piece I had hidden under the mattress. It doesn't matter—I can always find something. Paper clips stolen from the office, plastic silverware cracked just right, even a ragged fingernail can break the skin if you have the courage.

Alby faces the wall and traces imaginary coastlines on the white cement. She is dark and elfin, her hair shorn brutally close to her scalp except for one long tress that hangs behind her left ear. "Why do you wind him up like that?"

"Wind up who?" My voice is rough with disuse. Is it the next morning? Or have days passed? "And how?"

"Mr. L. The things you say to him . . ." Shuddering, Alby looks more wet terrier than girl. "If you'd just walk the line, I'm sure he'd leave you alone."

Having no memory of speaking to Mr. L at all, I just

shrug. "Walk the line. Walk the path. What's the difference?"

"Promise?"

"Okay."

"Yeah, play the game, let them think you're getting better." Alby straightens up, picturing home, I figure. She's got one to go back to. Wooden fence. Two-car garage. Mom and dad and a bowl full of breakfast cereal. No grandma making lemonade on a cold Sunday evening. No needles. No pins.

It's my turn to shudder. "I don't want to get better. They might send me home."

Alby stares at me. She has no answer to that. I turn to the bed. Start picking at the mattress, wondering if there are springs inside these old things. Alby faces the wall, her finger already winding a new path through the cracks. We all pass the time in our own way.

We get a new therapist the next day. We're always getting new ones. They stay a few weeks, a few months, and then gone.

This one wants us to write in journals. She gives us beautifully bound books, cloth covers with flowers and bunnies and unicorns and things, to put our ugly secrets in.

"Mine has Rainbow Brite." Alby is either excited or disgusted, I can't tell which.

Joelle says, "They should be snot colored. They should

be brown like . . ." She means shit. She never uses the word though.

"I want you to start thinking beautiful thoughts, Joelle," the therapist says. She has all our names memorized already. I think, *This one will only last two weeks. Long enough for us ruin the covers. Long enough for Joelle to rub her brown stuff on the pages.*

I put my hand on my own journal. It has these pretty flowers all over. I will write down my thoughts. But they won't be beautiful.

CUTTER
scissors
fillet knife
a broken piece of glass
I can't press hard enough
to do more than scratch the surface
and blood isn't red
until it touches the air

Okay, so it doesn't rhyme and I can't use it as a song, but it's true.

"What did you write, Red?" Alby asks.

Joelle has already left for the bathroom. I don't look forward to the smell from her book.

"Beautiful thoughts." I cover the poem with my hand. It *is* beautiful, I decide. Dark and beautiful, like I am when I dream.

"Little Red." Mr. L stands in the doorway. "Excuse me, Augustine. I need to see that one."

He points at me. I go away.

Four-footed and thick-furred, I stalk through a shadowy forest. My prey is just ahead of me—I can hear his ragged breathing, his terror-sweat. Long pink tongue to one side, I leap forward, galloping now. I burst through a flowering thornbush and catch sight of him: Mr. L, naked and covered in gray hair. I can smell his terror. Then I am on him, and my sharp teeth rip into his flesh. Bones crack and I taste marrow, sweet counterpoint to his salty blood.

I wake in the infirmary, arms and legs purple with fresh bruises.

"Jesus, Red," Alby says. "He really worked you over this time, didn't he?"

"I guess." I don't remember. Seems likely, though.

"Looks like you got him one too, though."

"Oh, yeah?" I can hardly move, though I turn my head toward the sound of her voice.

Alby grins her pixie smile. "Yeah. Got a big bandage on his neck, he does."

I lick my lips. Imagine I can taste blood. "Probably cut himself shaving."

Her smile fading, Alby says, "Whatever you say, Red."

I try to roll over, turn away from her, but something

holds me down: leather straps at my ankles and wrists. One across my waist.

"Five-point locked leather," Alby says, with some reverence. "You were really going crazy when they brought you in. Foaming at the mouth, even."

I lay my head back down on the small, hard pillow. Close my eyes. Maybe I can get back to my dream.

Mr. L visits me in the dark room with the leather straps. He has no bandage on his neck, but there are scratches there. I know why. I have his skin under my fingernails. In my teeth.

"Little Rojo," he says, almost lovingly, "you must learn control."

I try to laugh but all that comes out is a choking cough. He wanders slowly behind me, his fingers trailing through my red hair, my cap of blood.

"You must learn to walk the path." In front of me again, he glances up, at the television camera, the one that always watches. Puts his back to it.

"And will you be my teacher?" I ask before spitting at him.

He looks down at me. Smiles. "If you let me." Then he pats my cheek. Before he can touch me again, I go away.

The forest is cold that night and I stand on a forked road.

One is the path of needles, one the path of pins. I don't know which is which. Both are paths of pain.

I take the left.

I don't know how far I travel—what is distance to me? I am a night's walk from my den, a single leap from my next meal—but I am growing weary when the trap closes on my leg.

Sharp teeth and iron, it burns as it cuts. A howl escapes my throat, and I am thrown out of myself.

I see Mr. L standing over the strapped body of a girl. I can't see his hands. But I can feel them.

He looks up as I howl again, his face caught between pleasure and pain. I tumble through the thick walls and out into the cool night sky, into the dark forest, into my fur body.

I tear at my ankle with teeth made for the task. Seconds later, I leave my forepaw in the trap and limp back down the path.

It is days later. Weeks. Nighttime. Moon shining in my tiny window. They couldn't keep me tied down forever. The law doesn't allow it.

I am crouched in the corner of my room, ruined tube of toothpaste in my hands. I have figured out how to tear it, unwind it, form it into a razor edge. I hold it over my arm, scars glowing white in the moonlight, blue vein pulsing, showing me where to cut.

But I don't. Don't cut.

Instead I let the pain rise within me. I know one quick slash can end the pain. Can bring relief. But I don't move. I let the pain come and I embrace it, feel it wash over me, through me. I let it come—and then, I go away.

I am in the forest. But I am not four-footed. I am not thick-furred. I have no hope of tasting blood now or smelling the sweet scent of terrified prey.

I am me: scrawny and battered, short tufts of ragged red hair sprouting from my too-large head. Green eyes big. A gap between my top front teeth wide enough to escape through.

I stand in the middle of the road. No fork tonight: it runs straight and true like the surgeon's knife. Behind me, tall trees loom. I take two tentative steps and realize I am naked. Embarrassed, I glance around. I am alone.

Before long I see a white clapboard cottage ahead of me. Smoke trails from a red brick chimney. Gray paving stones lead up to the front door. I recognize the house. It is more threatening than the dark forest with its tall trees. Grandma lives here.

I turn to run, but behind me I hear howling—long, low, and mournful. I know the sound—wolves. Hunting wolves. I must hurry inside.

The door pulls open silently. The first room is unlit as I step inside. I pull the door closed behind me. Call into the darkness, "Grandma?"

"Is that you, Red?" Her voice is lower than I remember.

"Yes, Grandma." My voice shakes. My hands shake.

"Come into the bedroom. I can't hear you from here."

"I don't know the way, Grandma."

I hear her take a deep breath, thick with smoke, rattling with disease. "Follow my voice. You'll remember how."

And suddenly, I do remember. Three steps forward, nine steps left. Reach out with your right hand and push through the thin door.

"I am here, Grandma."

Outside, there are disappointed yips as the wolves reach the front door and the end of my trail.

"Come closer, Red. I can't see you from here."

"Yes, Grandma." I step into blackness and there she is, lying in the bed. She is bigger than I remember, or maybe I am smaller. The quilt puffs around her strangely, as if she has muscles in new places. A bit of drool dangles from her bottom lip.

I look down at my empty hands. My nakedness. "I haven't brought you anything, Grandma."

She smiles, showing bright, pointed teeth. "You have brought yourself, Red. Come closer, I can't touch you from here."

"Yes, Grandma." I take one step forward and stop.

The wolf pack snuffles around the outside of the house, searching for a way in.

Grandma sits up. Her skin hangs loosely on her, like a housedress a size too large. Tufts of fur poke out of her ears, rim her eyes.

"No, Grandma. You'll hurt me."

She shakes her head, and her face waggles loosely from

113

side to side. "I never hurt you, Red." She scrubs at her eye with a hairy knuckle, then scoots forward, crouching on the bed, poised to spring. Her haunches are thick and powerful. "Sometimes the wolf wears my skin. It is he who hurts you." Her nose is long now.

"No, Grandma." I stare into her dark green eyes. "No, Grandma. It's you."

She leaps then, her Grandma skin sloughing off as she flies for my throat. I turn and run, run through the thin door, run nine steps right and three steps back, push open the front door, hear her teeth snap behind me, severing tendons, bringing me down. I fall, collapsing onto the paving stones.

Howling and growling, a hundred wolves stream over and around me. Their padded feet are light on my body. They smell musty and wild. They take down Grandma in an instant, and I can hear her screams and the snapping of her brittle old bones.

I think I will die next, bleeding into the gray stone. But leathery skin grows over my ankle wound, thick gray fur. My nose grows cold and long and I smell Grandma's blood. Howling my rage and hunger, I leap to my four clawed feet. Soon, I am feasting on fresh meat with my brothers and sisters.

I wake, not surprised to be tied down again. Seven points this time, maybe more; I can't even move my head.

"Jesus, Red, you killed him this time." It is Alby, drifting into view above me.

"Go away, Alby. You aren't even real."

She nods without speaking and fades away. I go to sleep, I don't dream.

Next morning, they let me sit up. I ask for my journal. They don't want to give me a pen.

"You could hurt yourself," they say. "Cut yourself."

They don't understand.

"Then why don't *you* write down what I say," I tell them.

They laugh and leave me alone. Once again tied down. But I know what I want to write. It's all in my head.

GRANDMOTHER
What big ears you have,
What big teeth,
Big as scissors,
To cut out my heart
Pins and needles,
Needles and pins,
Where one life ends,
Another begins

WINTER'S KING

He was not born a king but the child of wandering players, slipping out ice-blue in the deepest part of winter, when the wind howled outside the little green caravan. The midwife pronounced him dead, her voice smoothly hiding her satisfaction. She had not wanted to be called to a birth on such a night.

But the father, who sang for pennies and smiles from strangers, grabbed the child from her and plunged him into a basin of lukewarm water, all the while singing a strange, fierce song in a tongue he did not really know.

Slowly the child turned pink in the water, as if breath were lent him by both the water and the song. He coughed once and spit up a bit of rosy blood, then wailed a note that was a minor third higher than his father's last surprised tone.

Without taking time to swaddle the child, the father laid him dripping wet and kicking next to his wife on the caravan bed. As she lifted the babe to her breast, the woman smiled at her husband, a look that included both the man and the child but cut the midwife cold.

The old woman muttered something that was part curse, part fear, then more loudly said, "No good will come of this dead cold child. He shall thrive in winter but never in the warm and he shall think little of this world. I have heard of such before. They are called Winter's Kin."

The mother sat up in bed, careful not to disturb the child at her side. "Then he shall be a Winter King, more than any of his kin or kind," she said. "But worry not, old woman, you shall be paid for the live child, as well as the dead." She nodded to her husband, who paid the midwife twice over from his meager pocket, six copper coins.

The midwife made the sign of horns over the money, but still she kept it and, wrapping her cloak tightly around her stout body and a scarf around her head, she walked out into the storm. Not twenty steps from the caravan, the wind tore the cloak from her and pulled tight the scarf about her neck. An icy branch broke from a tree and smashed in the side of her head. In the morning when she was found, she was frozen solid. The money she had clutched in her hand was gone.

The player was hanged for the murder and his wife left to mourn, even as she nursed the child. Then she married quickly, for the shelter and the food. Her new man never liked the winter babe.

"He is a cold one," the husband said. "He hears voices in the wind," though it was he who was cold and who, when filled with drink, heard the dark counsel of unnamed gods who told him to beat his wife and abuse her son. The woman never complained, for she feared for her child. Yet strangely the child did not seem to care. He paid more attention to the sounds of the wind than the shouts of his stepfather, lending his own voice to the cries he alone could hear, though always a minor third above.

As the midwife had prophesied, in winter he was an active child, his eyes bright and quick to laugh. But once spring came, the buds in his cheeks faded, even as the ones on the boughs grew big. In the summer and well into the fall, he was animated only when his mother told him tales of Winter's Kin, and though she made up the tales as only a player can, he knew the stories all to be true.

When the winter child was ten, his mother died of her brutal estate and the boy left into the howl of a storm, without either cloak or hat between him and the cold. Drunk, his ten-year father did not see him go. The boy did not go to escape the man's beatings; he went to his kin, who called him from the wind. Barefooted and bareheaded, he crossed the snows trying to catch up with the riders in the storm. He saw them clearly. They were clad in great white capes, the hoods lined with ermine; and when they turned to look at him, their eyes were wind blue and the bones of their faces were thin and fine.

Long, long he trailed behind them, his tears turned to ice. He wept not for his dead mother, for it was she who had tied him to the world. He wept for himself and his feet, which were too small to follow after the fast-riding Winter's Kin.

A woodcutter found him that night and dragged him home, plunging him into a bath of lukewarm water and speaking in a strange tongue that even he, in all his wanderings, had never heard.

The boy turned pink in the water, as if life had been returned to him by both the bathing and the prayer, but he did not thank the old man when he woke. Instead he turned his face to the window and wept, this time like any child, the tears falling like soft rain down his cheeks.

"Why do you weep?" the old man asked.

"For my mother and for the wind," the boy said. "And for what I cannot have."

The winter child stayed five years with the old woodcutter, going out each day with him to haul the kindling home. They always went into the woods to the south, a scraggly, ungraceful copse of second-growth trees, but never to the woods to the north.

"That is the great Ban Forest," the old man said. "All that lies therein belongs to the king."

"The king," the boy said, remembering his mother's tales. "And so I am."

"And so are we all in God's heaven," the old man said, "but here on earth I am a woodcutter and you are a found-ling boy. The wood to the south be ours."

Though the boy paid attention to what the old man

said in the spring and summer and fall, once winter arrived he heard only the voices in the wind. Often the old man would find him standing nearly naked by the door and have to lead him back to the fire, where the boy would sink down in a stupor and say nothing at all.

The old man tried to make light of such times, and would tell the boy tales while he warmed at the hearth. He told him of Mother Holle and her feather bed, of Godfather Death, and of the Singing Bone. He told him of the Flail of Heaven and the priest whose rod sprouted flowers because the Water Nix had a soul. But the boy had ears only for the voices in the wind, and what stories he heard there, he did not tell.

The old man died at the tag end of their fifth winter, and the boy left without even folding the hands of the corpse. He walked into the southern woods, for that was the way his feet knew. But the Winter Kin were not about.

The winds were gentle here, and spring had already softened the bitter brown branches to a muted rose. A yellow-green haze haloed the air and underfoot the muddy soil smelled moist and green and new.

The boy slumped to the ground and wept, not for the death of the woodcutter, nor for his mother's death, but for the loss once more of his kin. He knew it would be a long time 'til winter came again.

And then, from far away, he heard a final wild burst of music. A stray strand of cold wind snapped under his nose, as strong as a smelling bottle. His eyes opened wide and, without thinking, he stood.

Following the trail of song, as clear to him as cobbles on a city street, he moved toward the great Ban Forest, where the heavy trees still shadowed over winter storms. Crossing the fresh new furze between the woods, he entered the old dark forest and wound around the tall, black trees, in and out of shadows, going as true north as a needle in a water-filled bowl. The path grew cold and the once-muddy ground gave way to frost.

At first all he saw was a mist, as white as if the hooves of horses had struck up dust from sheer ice. But when he blinked once and then twice, he saw coming toward him a great company of fair folk, some on steeds the color of clouds and some on steeds the color of snow. And he realized all at once that it was no mist he had seen, but the breath of those great white stallions.

"My people," he cried at last. "My kin. My kind." And he tore off first his boots, then his trousers, and at last his shirt, until he was free of the world and its possessions and could run toward the Winter Kin naked and unafraid.

On the first horse was a woman of unearthly beauty. Her hair was plaited in a hundred white braids and on her head was a crown of diamonds and moonstones. Her eyes were wind blue and there was frost in her breath. Slowly she dismounted and commanded the stallion to be still. Then she took an ermine cape from across the saddle, holding it open to receive the boy.

"My king," she sang, "my own true love," and swaddled him in the cloud white cloak.

He answered her, his voice a minor third lower than hers. "My queen, my own true love. I am come home."

When the king's foresters caught up to him, the feathered arrow was fast in his breast, but there was, surprisingly, no blood. He was lying, arms outstretched, like an angel in the snow.

"He was just a wild boy, just that lackwit, the one who brought home kindling with the old man," said one.

"Nevertheless, he was in the king's forest," said the other. "He knew better than that."

"Naked as a newborn," said the first. "But look!"

In the boy's left hand were three copper coins, three more in his right.

"Twice the number needed for the birthing of a babe," said the first forester.

"Just enough," said his companion, "to buy a wooden casket and a man to dig the grave."

And they carried the cold body out of the wood, heeding neither the music nor the voices singing wild and strange hosannas in the wind.

INSCRIPTION

Father, they have burned your body,
Set your ashes in the cairn.
Still I need your advice.
Magnus sues for me in marriage,
Likewise McLeod of the three farms.
Yet would I wait for Iain the traveler,
Counting each step of his journey
Till the sun burns down behind Galan
Three and three hundred times;
Till he has walked to Steornabhagh
And back the long, hard track,
Singing my praises at every shieling
Where the lonely women talk to the east wind
And admire the ring he is bringing
To place on my small white hand.
          —Inscription on Callanish Stones, Isle of Lewis

It is a lie, you know, that inscription. From first to last. I did not want my father's advice. I had never taken it when he was alive, no matter how often he offered it. Still I need to confess what's been done.

If I do not die of this thing, I shall tell my son himself when he is old enough to understand. But if I cannot tell him, there will still be this paper to explain it: who his mother was, what she did for want of him, who and what his father was, and how the witch cursed us all.

Magnus Magnusson did ask for me in marriage, but he did not really want me. He did not want me though I was young and slim and fair. His eye was to the young men, but he wanted my father's farm and my father was a dying man, preferring a dram to a bannock.

And McLeod had the richest three farms along the machair, growing more than peat and sand. Still he was ugly and old, older even than my father, and as pickled, though his was of the brine where my father's was the whiskey.

Even Iain the traveler was no great catch, for he had no money at all. But ach—he was a lovely man, with hair the purple brown of heather in the spring or like a bruise beneath the skin. He was worth the loving but not worth the waiting for. Still I did not know it at the time.

I was nursed not by my mother, who died giving birth to me, but by brown-haired Mairi, daughter of Lachlan, who was my father's shepherd. And if she had married my father and given him sons, these troubles would not have come upon me. But perhaps that, too, is a lie. Even as a

child I went to trouble as a herring to the water, so Mairi
always said. Besides, my father was of that rare breed of
man who fancied only the one wife; his love once given
was never to be changed or renewed, even to the grave.

So I grew without a brother or sister to play with, a
trouble to my dear nurse and a plague to my father, though
neither ever complained of it. Indeed, when I stumbled in
the bog as the household dug the peat, and was near lost,
they dragged me free. When I fell down a hole in the cliff
when we went for birds' eggs, they paid a man from St.
Kilda's to rescue me with ropes. And when the sea herself
pulled me from the sands the day I went romping with the
selchies, they got in the big boat that takes four men and
a bowman in normal times, and pulled me back from the
clutching tide. Oh I was a trouble and a plague.

But never was I so much as when I came of age to
wed. That summer, after my blood flowed the first time
and Mairi showed me how to keep myself clean—and
no easy job of it—handsome Iain came through on his
wanderings. He took note of me I am sure, and not just
because he told me the summer after. A girl knows when
a man has an eye for her: she knows it by the burn of
her skin; she knows it by the ache in her bones. He said
he saw the promise in me and was waiting a year to collect on it. He had many such collections in mind, but I
wasn't to know.

His eyes were as purple-brown as his hair, like wild
plums. And his skin was dark from wandering. There is
not much sun on Leodhas, summer to winter, but if you
are constantly out in it, the wind can scour you. Iain the

traveler had that color; while others were red as rowan from the wind, he was brown as the roe. It made his teeth the whiter. It made the other men look boiled or flayed and laughable.

No one laughed at Iain. That is—no woman laughed at him.

So of course I loved him. How could I not? I who had been denied nothing by my father, nothing by my nurse. I loved Iain and wanted him, so I was certain to have him. How was I to know the count of days would be so short?

When he came through the next summer to collect on that promise, I was willing to pay. We met first on the long sea loch where I had gone to gather periwinkles and watch the boys come in from the sea, pulling on the oars of the boat, which made their new young muscles ripple.

Iain spoke to all of the women, few of the men, but for me he took out his whistle and played one of the old courting tunes. We had a laugh at that, all of us, though I felt a burn beneath my breastbone, by the heart, and could scarcely breathe.

I pretended he played the tune because I was watching out for the boys. He pretended he was playing it for Jennie Morrison, who was marrying Jamie Matheson before the baby in her belly swelled too big. But I already knew, really, he was playing just for me.

The pipes told me to meet him by the standing stones and so I did. He acted surprised to see me, but I knew he was not. He smoothed my hair and took me in his arms, and called me such sweet names as he kissed me I was sure I would die of it.

"Come tomorrow," he whispered, "when the dark finally winks," by which he meant well past midnight. And though I thought love should shout its name in the daylight as well as whisper at night, I did as he asked.

Sneaking from our house was not easy. Like most island houses, it was small and with only a few rooms, and the door was shared with the byre. But father and nurse and cows were all asleep, and I slipped out, barely stirring the peat smoke as I departed.

Iain was waiting for me by the stones, and he led me down to a place where soft grasses made a mat for my back. And there he taught me the pain of loving as well as the sweetness of it. I did not cry out, though it was not from wanting. But bred on the island means being strong, and I had only lately given over playing shinty with the boys. Still there was blood on my legs and I cleaned myself with grass and hurried back as the sun—what there was of it—was rising, leaving Iain asleep and guarded by the stones.

If Mairi noticed anything, she said nothing. At least not that day. And as I helped her at the quern preparing meal, and gave a hand with the baking as well, all the while

suppressing the yawns that threatened to expose me, perhaps she did not know.

When I went back to the stones that night, Iain was
waiting for me and this time there was neither blood nor
pain, though I still preferred the kisses to what came after.

But I was so tired that I slept beside him all that night,
or what was left of it. At dawn we heard the fishermen
calling to one another as they passed by our little nest
on the way to their boats. They did not see us: Iain knew
how to choose his places well. Still I did not rise, for no
fisherman dares meet a woman as he goes toward the sea
for fear of losing his way in the waves. So I was forced to
huddle there in the shelter of Iain's arms 'til the fishermen—some of them the boys I had lately played shinty
with—were gone safely on their way.

This time when I got home Mairi was already up at the
quern, her face as black as if it had been rinsed in peat. She
did not say a word to me, which was even worse, but by
her silence I knew she had said nothing to my father, who
slept away in the other room.

That was the last but one I saw of Iain that summer, though
I went night after night to look for him at the stones. My
eyes were red from weeping silently as I lay in the straw by
Mairi's side, and she snoring so loudly, I knew she was not
really asleep.

I would have said nothing, but the time came around
and my blood did not flow. Mairi knew the count of it

since I was so new to womanhood. Perhaps she guessed even before I did, for I saw her looking at me queer. When I felt queasy and was sick behind the house, there was no disguising it.

"Who is it?" she asked. Mairi was never one for talking too much.

"Iain the traveler," I said. "I am dying for love of him."

"You are not dying," she said, "lest your father kill you for this. We will go to Auld Annie who lives down the coast. She practices the black arts and can rid you of the child."

"I do not want to be rid of it," I said. "I want Iain."

"He is walking out with Margaret MacKenzie in her shieling. Or if not her, another."

"Never! He loves me," I said. "He swore it."

"He loves," Mairi said, purposefully coarse to shock me, "the cherry in its blossom but not the tree. And his swearing is done to accomplish what he desires."

She took me by the hand, then, before I could recover my tongue, and we walked half the morning down the strand to Auld Annie's croft, it being ten miles or so by. There was only a soft, fair wind and the walking was not hard, though we had to stop every now and again for me to be quietly sick in the sand.

Auld Annie's cottage was much the smallest and meanest I had seen. Still it had a fine garden both in front and again in back in the long rig. Plants grew there in profusion, in lazy beds, and I had no name for many of them.

"She can call fish in by melted lead and water," Mairi said. "She can calm the seas with seven white stones."

I did not look impressed, but it was my stomach once more turning inside me.

"She foretold your own dear mother's death."

I looked askance. "Why didn't I know of this?"

"Your father forbade me ever speak of it."

"And now?"

"Needs does as needs must." She knocked on the door.

The door seemed to open of itself because when we got inside, Auld Annie was sitting far from it, in a rocker, a coarse black shawl around her shoulders and a mutch tied under her chin like any proper wife. The croft was lower and darker than ours, but there was a broad mantel over the fire and on it sat two piles of white stones with a human skull, bleached and horrible, staring at the wall between them. On the floor by a long table were three jugs filled with bright red poppies, the only color in the room. From the rafters hung bunches of dried herbs, but they were none of them familiar to me.

Under her breath, Mairi muttered a charm:

I trample 'pon the eye
As tramples the duck 'pon the lake,
In the name of the secret Three,
And Brigid the Bride . . .

and made a quick sign against the *Droch Shùil,* the evil eye.

"I knew it, I knew ye were coming, Molly," Auld Annie said.

How she knew that—or my name—I could not guess.

"I knew it as I knew when yer mam was going to die."
Her voice was low, like a man's.

"We haven't come for prophecy," I said.

"Ye have come about a babe."

My jaw must have gone agape at that for I had told no
one but Mairi and that only hours before. Surely Auld Annie was a witch, though if she threw no shadow one could
not tell in the dark of her house. Nevertheless I shook my
head. "I will keep the babe. All I want is the father to come
to me."

"Coming is easy," Auld Annie said in her deep voice.
"Staying is hard."

"If you get him to come to me," I answered, suddenly
full of myself, "I will get him to stay."

From Mairi there was only a sharp intake of breath in
disapproval, but Auld Annie chuckled at my remark, dangerous and low.

"Come then, girl," she said, "and set yer hand to my
churn. We have butter to take and spells to make and a
man to call to yer breast."

I did not understand entirely, but I followed her to the
churn, where she instructed me in what I had to do.

"As ye churn, girl, say this: *Come, butter, come. Come,
butter, come.*"

"I know this charm," I said witheringly. "I have since a
child."

"Ah—but instead 'a saying 'butter,' ye must say yer man's
name. Only—" she raised her hand in warning, "not aloud.
And ye must not hesitate even a moment's worth between
the words. Not once. Ye must say it over and over 'til the

131

butter be done. It is not easy, for all it sounds that way."

I wondered—briefly—if all she was needing was a strong young girl to do her chores, but resolved to follow her instructions. It is a dangerous thing to get a witch angry with you. And if she could call Iain to me, so much the better.

So I put my hands upon the churn and did as she bid, over and over and over without a hesitation 'til my arms ached and my mind was numb and all I could hear was Iain's name in my head, the very sound of it turning my stomach and making me ill. Still I did not stop 'til the butter had come.

Auld Annie put her hands upon mine, and they were rough and crabbed with time. "Enough!" she said, "or it will come sour as yer belly, and we will have done all for nought."

I bit back the response that it was not we but I who had done the work and silently put my aching arms down at my sides. Only then did I see that Annie herself had not been idle. On her table lay a weaving of colored threads.

"A framing spell," Mairi whispered by my side. "A *deilbh buidseachd.*"

I resisted crossing myself and spoiling the spell and went where Annie led me, to the rocking chair.

"Sit ye by the fire," she said.

No sooner had I sat down, rubbing my aching arms and trying not to jump up and run outside to be sick, when a piece of the peat broke off in the hearth and tumbled out at my feet.

"Good, good," Auld Annie crooned. "Fire bodes marriage. We will have success."

I did not smile. Gritting my teeth, I whispered, "Get on with it."

"Hush," cautioned Mairi, but her arms did not ache as mine did.

Auld Annie hastened back to the churn and, dipping her hand into it, carved out a pat of butter the size of a shinty ball with her nails. Slapping it down on the table by the threads, she said: "Name three colors, girl, and their properties."

"Blue like the sea by Galan's Head," I said.

"Good, good, two more."

"Plum—like his eyes."

"And a third."

I hesitated, thinking. "White," I said at last. "White—like . . . like God's own hair."

Auld Annie made a loud tch sound in the back of her throat and Mairi, giving a loud, explosive exhalation, threw her apron up over her head.

"Not a proper choice, girl," Auld Annie muttered. "But what's said cannot be unsaid. Done is done."

"Is it spoiled?" I whispered.

"Not spoiled. Changed." She drew the named colors of thread from the frame and laid them, side by side, across the ball of butter. "Come here,"

I stood up and went over to her, my arms all a-tingle.

"Set the two threads at a cross for the name of God ye so carelessly invoked, and one beneath for yer true love's name."

I did as she bid, suddenly afraid. What had I called up

133

or called down, so carelessly in this dark house?

Auld Annie wrapped the butter in a piece of yellowed linen, tying the whole up with a black thread, before handing it to me.

"Take this to the place where ye wish to meet him and bury it three feet down, first drawing out the black thread. Cover it over with earth and while doing so recite three times the very words ye said over the churn. He will come that very evening. He will come—but whether he will stay is up to ye, my girl."

I took the sachet in my right hand and dropped it carefully into the pocket of my apron.

"Come now, girl, give me a kiss to seal it."

When I hesitated, Mairi pushed me hard in the small of the back and I stumbled into the old woman's arms. She smelled of peat and whiskey and age, not unlike my father, but there was something more I could put no name to. Her mouth on mine was nothing like Iain's, but was bristly with an old woman's hard whiskers and her lips were cracked. Her sour breath entered mine and I reeled back from her, thankful to be done. As I turned, I glanced at the mantel. To my horror I saw that between the white stones, the skull was now facing me, its empty sockets black as doom.

Mairi opened the cottage door and we stumbled out into the light, blinking like hedgehogs. I started down the path, head down. When I gave a quick look over my shoulder, Mairi was setting something down by Auld Annie's door. It was a payment, I knew, but for what and how much I did not ask, then or ever.

We walked back more slowly than we had come, and I chattered much of the way, as if the charming had been on my tongue to loosen it. I told Mairi about Iain's hair and his eyes and every word he had spoken to me, doling them out a bit at a time because, truth to tell, he had said little. I recounted the kisses and how they made me feel and even—I blush to think of it now—how I preferred them to what came after. Mairi said not a word in return until we came to the place where the path led away to the standing stones.

When I made to turn, she put her hand on my arm. "No, not there," she said. "I told you he has gone up amongst the shielings. If you want him to come to you, I will have your father send you up to the high pasture today."

"He will come wherever I call him," I said smugly, patting the pocket where the butter lay.

"Do not be more brainless than you have been already," Mairi said. "Go where you have the best chance of making him stay."

I saw at last what she meant. At the stones we would have to creep and hide and lie still lest the fishermen spy us. We would have to whisper our love. But up in the high pasture, along the cliffside, in a small croft of our own, I could bind him to me by night and by day, marrying him in the old way. And no one—especially my father—could say no to such a wedding.

So Mairi worked her own magic that day, much more

homey than Auld Annie's, with a good hot soup and a hearty dram and a word in the ear of my old father. By the next morning she had me packed off to the shieling, with enough bannocks and barley and flasks of water in my basket to last me a fortnight, driving five of our cows before.

The cows knew the way as well as I, and they took to the climb like weanlings, for the grass in the shieling was sweet and fresh and greener than the overgrazed land below. In another week Mairi and I would have gone up together. But Mairi had my father convinced that I was grown enough to make the trip for the first time alone. Grown enough—if he had but known!

Perhaps it was the sea breeze blowing on my face, or the fact that I knew Iain would be in my arms by dark. Or perhaps it was just that the time for such sickening was past, but I was not ill at all on that long walk, my step as jaunty as the cows'.

It was just coming on late supper when we turned off the path to go up and over the hill to the headland where our little summer croft sits. The cows followed their old paths through the matted bog with a quiet satisfaction, but I leaped carelessly from tussock to tuft behind them.

I walked—or rather danced—to the cliff's edge where the hummocks and bog and gray-splattered stone gave way to the sheer of cliff. Above me the gannets flew high and low, every now and again veering off to plummet into the sea after fish. A solitary seal floated below, near some rocks, looking left, then right, then left again but never once up at me.

With the little hoe I had brought along for the purpose, I dug a hole, fully three feet down, and reverently laid in the butter pat. Pulling the black thread from the sachet, I let the clods of dirt rain back down on it, all the while whispering, "Come, Iain, come. Come, Iain, come." Then loudly I sang out, "Come, Iain, come!" without a hesitation in between. Then I packed the earth down and stood, rubbing the small of my back where Mairi had pushed me into the sealing kiss.

I stared out over the sea, waiting.

He did not come until past dark, which in summer is well in to the mid of the night. By then I had cooked myself a thin barley gruel, and made the bed up, stuffing it with soft grasses and airing out the croft.

I heard his whistle first, playing a raucous courting tune, not the one he had played on the beach when first I had noticed him, but "The Cuckoo's Nest," with words that say the one thing, but mean another.

In the dim light it took him a minute to see me standing by the door. Then he smiled that slow, sure smile of his. "Well . . . Molly," he said.

I wondered that he hesitated over my name, almost as if he could not recall it, though it had been but a few short weeks before that he had whispered it over and over into my tumbled hair.

"Well, Iain," I said. "You have come to me."

"I have been called to you," he said airily. "I could not stay away."

And then suddenly I understood that he did not know there was magic about; that these were just words he spoke, part of his lovemaking, that meant as little to him as the kisses themselves, just prelude to his passion.

Well, I had already paid for his pleasure and now he would have to stay for mine. I opened my arms and he walked into them as if he had never been away, his kisses the sweeter now that I knew what he was and how to play his game.

In the morning I woke him with the smell of barley bread. I thought if I could get him to stay a second night, and a third, the charm would have a chance of really working. So I was sweet and pliant and full of an ardor that his kisses certainly aroused, though that which followed seemed to unaccountably dampen it. Still, I could dissemble when I had to, and each time we made love I cried out as if fulfilled. Then while he slept, I tiptoed out to the place where I had buried the butter sachet.

"Stay, Iain, stay. Stay, Iain, stay," I recited over the little grave where my hopes lay buried.

For a day and another night it seemed to work. He did stay—and quite happily—often sitting half-dressed in the cot watching me cook or lying naked on the sandy beach, playing his whistle to call the seals to him. They rose up out of the water, gazing long at him, as if they were bewitched.

We made love three and four and five times, day and night, 'til my thighs ached the way my arms had at the churn, and I felt scrubbed raw from trying to hold on to him.

But on the third day, when he woke, he refused both the barley and my kisses.

"Enough, sweet Moll," he said. "I am a traveler, and I must travel." He got dressed slowly, as if almost reluctant to leave but satisfying the form of it. I said nothing 'til he put his boots on, then could not stop myself.

"On to another shieling, then?"

"Perhaps."

"And what of the babe—here." It was the first time I had mentioned it. From the look on his face, I knew it made no matter to him, and without waiting for an answer, I stalked out of the croft. I went to the headland and stood athwart the place where the butter lay buried.

"Stay, Iain," I whispered. "Stay . . . ," but there was neither power nor magic nor desire in my calling.

He came up behind me and put his arms around me, crossing his hands over my belly where the child-to-be lay quiet.

"Marry another," he whispered, nuzzling my ear, "but call him after me."

I turned in his arms and pulled him around to kiss me, my mouth wide open as if to take him in entire. And when the kiss was done, I pulled away and pushed him over the cliff into the sea.

Like most men of Leodhais, he could not swim, but little it would have availed him, for he hit the rocks and then the water, sinking at once. He did not come up again 'til three seals pushed him ashore onto the beach, where they huddled by his body for a moment as if expecting a tune, then plunged back into the sea when there was none.

I hurried down and cradled his poor broken body in my arms, weeping not for him but for myself and what I had lost, what I had buried up on that cliff, along with the butter, in a boggy little grave. Stripping the ring from his hand, I put it on my own, marrying us in the eyes of the sea. Then I put him on my back and carried him up the cliffside to bury him deep beneath the heather that would soon be the color of his hair, of his eyes.

Two weeks later, when Mairi came, I showed her the ring.

"We were married in God's sight," I said, "with two selchies as bridesmaids and a gannet to cry out the prayers."

"And where is the bridegroom now?" she asked.

"Gone to Steornabhagh," I lied, "to whistle us up money for our very own croft." She was not convinced. She did not say so, but I could read her face.

Of course he never returned and—with Mairi standing up for me—I married old McLeod after burying my father, who had stumbled into a hole one night after too much whiskey, breaking both his leg and his neck.

McLeod was too old for more than a kiss and a cuddle—as Mairi had guessed—and too pigheaded to claim the child wasn't his own. When the babe was born hale and whole, I named him Iain, a common-enough name in these parts, with only his nurse Mairi the wiser. At McLeod's death a year later, I gave our old farm over to her. It was a payment, she knew, but exactly for what she never asked, not then or ever.

Now I lie abed with the pox, weakening each day, and would repent of the magic and the rest—though not of the loving which gave me my child. Still I would have my Iain know who his mother was and what she did for want of him, who and what his father was, and how the witch cursed us all. I would not have my son unmindful of his inheritance. If ever the wind calls him to travel, if ever a witch should tempt him to magic, or if ever a cold, quiet rage makes him choose murder, he will understand and, I trust, set all those desires behind.

Written this year of Our Lord 1539, Tir a' Gheallaidh, Isle of Lewis

DOG BOY
REMEMBERS

The Dog Boy was just a year old and newly walking when his father returned to take him into Central Park. It was summer and the moon was full over green trees.

The only scents he'd loved 'til then were the sweet milk smells his mother made, the fust of the sofa cushions, the prickly up-your-nose of the feathers in his pillow, the pure spume of water from the tap, and the primal stink of his own shit before it was washed down into the white bowl.

When his father came to fetch him that first time, his mother wept. Still in her teens, she'd not had a lot of knowledge of the world before Red Cap had taken her up. But the baby, he was all hers. *The only thing*, she often thought, *that truly was.*

"Don't take him," she cried, "I've done everything you asked. I promise to be even more careful of him." Her tears slipped silently down her cheeks, small globules, smelling slightly salty, like soup.

His father hit her with his fist for crying, and red blood gushed from her nose. He hated crying, something Dog Boy was soon to find out.

But Dog Boy had never smelled blood like that before, only his mother's monthly flow which had a nasty pong to it. His head jerked up at the sharpness, a scent he would later know as iron. He practically wet himself with delight.

His father watched him and smiled. It was a slow smile and not at all comforting, but it was all Dog Boy would ever get from him.

"Come, Boy," his father said, adjusting the red cap he always wore, a cap that was the first thing Dog Boy recognized about his father, even before his smell, that odd compound of old blood and something meaty, something nasty, that both repelled and excited him. Without more of an invitation, his father reached into his pocket and pulled out a leather leash, winding it expertly about the Dog Boy's chest and shoulders, tugging him toward the door. And not knowing why, only that it would surely be something new and interesting, Dog Boy toddled after him, never looking back at his mother who still simpered behind them.

Off they went into the city, that big, noisy, sprawling place so full of sound and movement and smells. Dog Boy always shuddered when the door opened.

Oh, he'd been out with his mother before, but always held in her arms, smothered by the milk-mother smell. This time he was walking out on his own. Well, walking might be a slight exaggeration. It was more like falling forward, only to be caught up again and again by the leather leash.

Their first stop was at a spindly gingko right outside the door of the house, the tree just leafing out. Dog Boy stood by it and inhaled the green, soft and sharp at the same time. He reached over and touched the bark. That was the soft smell, and it was not—he realized in surprise—the bark itself but the mallow he could sense inside, though of course then he hadn't the words *mallow* or *bark*. The leaves were what smelled sharp and new and somewhat peppery. The other smell was clearly much older. Old and new had different scents. It was a revelation.

Next, he and his father walked along a stone walk that was filled with other interesting scents. People smells, lingering leather smells, the sweat of feet, plus the sweet cloy of dropped paper wrappers, and some smallish tangs of tobacco in a white cover. Then Dog Boy found three overflowing garbage cans, overflowing with smells.

Suddenly, there were far too many odors, most of them much too strong for his childish senses, and Dog Boy ended up swooning onto the pavement, his legs and arms making quick running motions, like a dog does when it dreams.

With great disgust, Red Cap slung him over his shoulder like some dead thing, and took him right back home.

Once upstairs, he flung Dog Boy onto the sofa, saying in his growl of a voice, "I have kept you in comfort all this time and you raise up this . . . this wimpish thing. I need a sniffer-out, an offspring who can track and trail. Not this puling. Fainting—"

"He's only a baby," his mother said quickly, picking Dog Boy up and unwrapping the leather leash from his body which—strangely—burned her hands. Dog Boy smelled the burning right before she cradled him against her milk-full breasts, before that familiar scent comforted him and made him forget everything else. "And I have kept him in this room, as you demanded . . ." his mother murmured above him, neglecting to mention the bi-weekly runs to the bodega when she was so lonely for an adult to speak to, she couldn't stay in and didn't dare leave the child in the room alone.

For her outburst, she was hit again, this time on the cheek, which rocked her back and made Dog Boy whimper for her, though she made no sound at all. But her cheek came up quickly into a purplish bruise that his little, plump fingers explored gently, though by then Red Cap was already gone, the door slamming behind him. He didn't return for a month, on the next moon.

During that month, Dog Boy's mother wept, fussed, petted, and spoiled him outrageously, thought about running, hiding out somewhere.

"Just the two of us," she'd whisper before the tears pooled again in her eyes. "Anywhere." But she couldn't think of a single place that would be safe. Red Cap could come and go to anywhere on earth, seemingly at will. He'd told her so when they'd first met, and she believed him. His fists had made her into a believer.

Red Cap was the only name she had for him. He said it was the only name he had. She'd tried calling him Red once, and he'd hit her so hard, she lost consciousness and never tried again. Even her father had never hit her so hard. But after that, she had trouble calling him anything and spent stuttering moments whenever she had to address him directly. She thought if she could only call him by his right name, he'd forgive her, but the words never seemed to come out right.

He wore that disgusting cap everywhere, even in bed. The only time she'd ever seen him take it off was when they were first seeing one another. It was a pearly evening, and they'd come upon a dying squirrel run over in the park, its insides squashed onto the pavement, made even more horrible by the moon overhead and the shadows it cast. She'd started to turn away from the sight. But when Red Cap took off his hat and dipped it into the squirrel's blood, she'd been mesmerized and couldn't stop watching. For a moment, the hat had seemed to glisten and glow, red as a sunset, though she knew that couldn't really have happened. Then the squirrel's eyes glazed over; so in a way, had the hat.

After the moment in the park, she shrank away from him, which seemed to make him even more ardent. He showered her with money. Especially when he found out she was pregnant. He didn't ask her to marry him, but by then marriage was the last thing on her mind. Escape was foremost. That and getting rid of the child in her womb. But Red Cap stayed with her, imprisoned her really, in that little house in Brooklyn, with its view of the backside of another building. Threatened her. Hit her a couple of times a week just to remind her he could. He knew how to draw blood and how to bring bruises. He did not mistake them. It was as if he knew her body better than she did. And her soul.

He stayed just long enough for the child to be born. Childbirth tore her up so badly inside, the doctor warned she'd never have another child, though she didn't want another. Certainly not with Red Cap.

When she was well enough to take care of the child on her own, he showed her what to do, and then left, warning her not to run away.

"I can find you wherever you go," he'd said. "I'll be back when he is walking." She believed him.

The money he paid her with—it came in brown envelopes stuffed under the door—was generous and arrived mysteriously after she was asleep. But it had to be given to a bank first thing in the morning because by midnight it turned into leaves or ashes or bits of colored paper. So he'd warned her, and she knew that to be true because once she'd kept an envelope a second night, first checking that it was full of the promised money. When she opened the envelope the next morning, it was filled with red and gold autumn leaves instead. And so she'd nothing for almost a month and had to go back to tricking to keep the baby and herself alive.

Predictably, Red Cap had beaten her when he returned.

Somehow he'd known what she'd done without having to ask.

"It's written on your stupid cow face," he told her, and flung another envelope at her. He never asked about the child.

After that, she went early to the bank, the baby bound up tightly to her breast so that he didn't smell anything but her and the milk, just as Red Cap had demanded. Of course, every few months she had to change banks, but since Red Cap continued his generosity that made it only a small burden.

Of course she grew to love the child, who looked nothing like either one of them but had a dark feral beauty and a brilliant smile. He seemed content being in the little apartment, entranced by the television Red Cap's money had purchased, and absolutely stunned by the music he heard there. She bought him a little pipe that he tootled on incessantly, and soon was able to mimic bird songs, and so she named him Robin after her favorite bird. His father refused to use that name, continuing to call him Dog Boy, which she hated.

One time she shorted herself on food and bought Robin a small tape CD player along with a variety of CDs: Battlefield Band, Janis Ian, Steeleye Span, the Silly Sisters—all favorites of hers. None of this new stuff. Except for Amanda Palmer and the Dixie Chicks. He begged then for a fiddle, and she went on short rations for several months 'til she had enough to buy it for him, a quarter-size fiddle that he taught himself to play.

And she talked to the child constantly. Well, she had to.

didn't she? There was no one else to talk to except when they went quickly to the bank or to the local bodega at the end of the road. She kept herself busy during the day with the boy—playing with him, singing to him, washing his clothes, teaching him numbers, nursery rhymes, dreaming of escape.

But Red Cap came back as she knew he would. As he'd warned he would.

He put a stupid strap around the boy's shoulders and chest. Then off they went, her little boy trotting along in that new, funny, rolling sailor walk behind him and Red Cap yanking on the leash as if Robin had been a dog and not a human boy.

Of course Robin was a disappointment to his father. So he worked harder at trying to please him. He learned the smells of the city as if they were his ABCs. Graduating from milk and mother to finger foods and distinguishing gingko from maple. Learned the difference between sandals, shoes, and sneakers. Then the differences between Nikes, Pumas, Reeboks; between Kurt Geigers, and Crocs; between Doc Martens, Jimmy Choos, Manolo Blahniks, Mephisto, and Birkenstocks. Though it would be years before he had names for the shoes, just the smells.

By the time he was four, he was able to follow a woman down a street an hour after she'd walked by without ever seeing her, simply by the smell of her Jimmy Choos and the waft of perfume.

By the time he was six, he could track two men at the same time, and when they parted, he could find one, mark that territory with his own personal scent (a piece of chewing gum, a wipe of his hand over his hair, which was now long and shaggy as a dog's, or even by peeing around the spot if no one was watching). Then he'd go back to the place of parting, and track the second.

The praise he got from his father was little enough.

It felt enormous.

"It's time," Red Cap told the boy on his tenth birthday.

Dog Boy knew what he meant without having to be told. He was well-trained. He was old enough. He'd long been off the leash. This day he would be in at a kill. A blooding, his father called it. He couldn't wait.

His father handed him a small child's cap. It was a school cap, blue with an insignia, a red pine tree and the numbers 1907. He sniffed it. He would know that scent anywhere.

They walked to a small park, a kind of grove. It was filled with lovely smells that made Dog Boy shiver with delight. The sharp, new growing things, both white-rooted and green. Little mealy-smelling worms. The deep musk of the old oak's serpentine roots that lay halfway above ground.

There were many sneaker smells, too, mostly the rubbery scent that made *his* nose itch. But there was a familiar odor, faint but clear enough for him to follow.

He lifted his right hand and pointed at a place where the path forked. Eager to be off, he was stopped by his father's rough grasp on his shirt collar.

"Now is when we must take care," Red Cap told him. "Be subtle. Act like everyday humankind. An ordinary father and his ordinary son on an outing. Not a hunter and his dog." Though there was nothing ordinary about the pair.

Dog Boy nodded; he could scarcely contain his excitement. His father had spoken quietly, not in his usual sharp trainer's voice, nor in his dangerous growl. Dog Boy liked this new, quiet, unexpected sound. It soothed him. It calmed him down.

"Steady, steady now. Show me the way." Red Cap took his son's hand.

This was so unusual. Dog Boy almost stopped to say something, then thought better of it and went on.

They walked along, almost companionably, and any onlooker would have no reason to think they were not a happy pair out for a Sunday stroll. When they reached the fork, the smell drew Dog Boy to the left. And then another left. And because his father still had hold of his hand, he was drawn along as well. They came into a small, hidden, grassy place where dark trees bent nearly double.

A boy, younger than Dog Boy, was standing, his back to them. By the way he stood, Dog Boy knew he'd come into this out-of-the-way place to pee.

"Let him finish," whispered his father. "We have time." As an afterthought, almost as if laughing at the child, he added, "Though he does not."

Dog Boy wondered: *Time for what?* But deep inside he knew, had always known, had tried to keep himself from knowing. For him, it was the seeking, the finding that mattered. But not for his father. Never for his father. He shuddered.

They moved closer to the boy who, turning, looked a bit alarmed, then relieved, then frightened, then terrified. Then silent.

Dog Boy couldn't stop staring. There was blood everywhere. The sharp iron tang got up his nose as if it had painted itself there. He wondered if he would ever smell anything else.

Watching his father dip the red cap in the boy's blood, he tried to weep. He tried to turn away. He could do neither.

They walked in silence back to the house. A tall black boy his age ran by, his legs scissoring. A smaller kid, maybe a brother, cried after him, "Chim, Chim, wait for me."

The bigger boy stopped, turned, caught the little one up in his arms, swung him onto his shoulders. "Hold tight!" he said. "Don't want you to fall." Then off he trotted, the little one's legs wrapped around his arms, his small hands in his brother's afro. Their gales of laughter floated back to Dog Boy, who shrugged himself further into his own shoulders, as if he might disappear there. Had he ever laughed that way? Maybe with his mother, once or twice, certainly never with his father. He pictured himself swinging a small child up on his shoulders, the weight of the child, the laughter. He imagined trotting along the park path, the wind blowing the scent of lilac and azalea, the smell sweet, not cloying. Both child and laughter were light in his reverie.

At that moment, Dog Boy had forgotten what his father looked like dipping his cap in the slaughtered boy's blood. How his face had changed into some sort of . . . creature: *An orc, maybe. Or a troll*, he'd thought at the time, pulling monsters from his reading. A smiling monster. But in the wake of the two laughing boys, he couldn't retain the horror of the child's blood. The memory of Chim and his brother—Dog Boy was suddenly sure it was a brother—that memory was even stronger than the memory of the dead child. He couldn't think why.

Once home, the image of the murdered boy returned to him, as well as the smell of it so he went immediately into the bathroom where he washed his face and hands obsessively for what seemed like hours though in fact it was just ten minutes. Then he took out the neti pot his father made him use whenever they were about to go out on a practice run. The warm water through his nose and nasal passages flushed away the lingering blood scent and the last of the memory of the dead boy. He would remember the day as the one where he saw the black boys and their joy with one another.

When he joined his father in the living room, Red Cap

was standing awkwardly, staring at the sofa where Dog Boy's mother sprawled. Neither one of them was moving.

Something in the room was strange. It smelled off. Muted. Cold.

Dog Boy ran over to the sofa and looked down at his mother's face. All the lines in it had been oddly smoothed out. She looked almost happy. She smelled . . . For a moment, he had no name for it. And then he had it.

Peaceful.

Then realizing what that meant, he threw himself across her body and began to weep.

When the weeping was over and he had no more tears to cry, he picked her up in his arms as if she were a child, and the bottle of pills she'd been clutching in one hand shook loose.

He turned to look up at his father, to ask him what had happened. Why it had happened.

Red Cap was smiling. It was—Dog Boy thought—the same smile he'd stretched across his mouth when sopping up the murdered child's blood.

"Now I can take you to the Greenwood," Red Cap said. "Nothing holds you here anymore."

Dog Boy opened his mouth. For a minute no sound came out. Finally, as if it was a truth that needed telling, he said quietly, "*She* holds me here."

"*She* is dead," Red Cap said as if the boy hadn't the sense to realize it on his own. "And not even blood for the dipping."

That was when Dog Boy first understood how much he hated his father. How much he hated being his father's dog. He set his mother's body down on the couch again, carefully, as if afraid he might bring her back from her final escape. Taking the small crocheted quilt that hung on the sofa's arm, he covered her with it. She looked tiny, small, and—suddenly—safe.

"I'm staying."

"You cannot."

Dog Boy made his hands into fists. More tears began to roll down his face. He expected to be beaten. It would not be the first time. Probably not the last. He was prepared for it.

What he was not prepared for, though, was his father reaching into a pocket and taking out the leash, which Dog Boy hadn't seen in years. Quickly, Red Cap bound him as easily and as tightly as he'd ever done when Dog Boy had been a child.

For the first time Dog Boy could actually feel the leash's power. Perhaps he felt it because he didn't want to go where it willed him, where his father willed him. Always before he'd been eager to go outside, to smell the city scents, to do what his father would have him do. When he'd been little, he thought that the leash was only to keep him safe. He'd been proud the day he was old enough to go outside with Red Cap leashless. He believed he and his father had forged a team: two hunters, leaning on one another. He had the nose, his father kept him safe. Equals. He'd reveled in that.

But now he understood the truth. The leash was not just a piece of leather to keep him from getting lost, to keep him out of harm's way. There was something else about it. Something that glimmered on the inside. Something fierce. Something old that he was powerless to resist.

Red Cap pulled on the leash and it drew Dog Boy relentlessly toward the door.

"I want my fiddle and pipe." His voice was high, but not pleading. He would not make his mother's mistake. Pleading just gave his father some kind of strange pleasure.

"You'll not need it where we're going."

"Where is that?"

"Under the Hill."

For a moment he thought his father meant underground. It was something he'd watched on a TV show: a family on the run from the mafia had to go underground to escape certain death. Perhaps, he thought, his father meant the child they killed was the son of a mafia chieftain, or maybe the child of a policeman. Or the FBI.

Underground. They'd be on the run. Together.

But then he remembered the smile, the dipped hat, the blood, the obvious pleasure that his father had taken in the stalking, the killing of an innocent child. And he remembered something else. His father—for all that he was a bloodthirsty, vicious murderer—never lied. They were going Under the Hill, whatever that meant.

Looking back at his mother's body on the sofa, wrapped in the red and green coverlet, at the silver pipe on the table, at the fiddle in its case resting against the wall, Dog Boy told himself: Someday I will kill him for this. Once more the murdered boy was all but forgotten. By *this*, he meant his mother's suicide.

When I am old enough and big enough and strong enough,

he will pay for this. Then I will take the red cap and dip it in his blood.

He wondered if this was just a boy's wish or whether it was a promise.

"A pledge," he whispered.

Like his father, he did not lie.

THE FISHERMAN'S WIFE

John Merton was a fisherman. He brought up eels and elvers, little finny creatures and great sharp-toothed monsters from the waves. He sold their flesh at markets and made necklaces of their teeth for the fairs.

If you asked him, he would say that what he loved about the ocean was its vast silence, and wasn't that why he had married him a wife the same. Deaf she was, and mute too, but she could talk with her hands, a flowing syncopation. He would tell you that, and it would be no lie. But there were times when he would go mad with her silences, as the sea can drive men mad, and he would leave the house to seek the babble of the marketplace. As meaningful as were her finger fantasies, they brought his ear no respite from the quiet.

There was one time, though, that he left too soon, and it happened this way. It was a cold and gray morning, and he slammed the door on his wife, thinking she would not know it, forgetting there are other ways to hear. And as he walked along the shore, singing loudly to himself—so as to prime his ears—and swinging the basket of fish pies he had for the fair, he heard only the sound of his own voice. The hush of the waves might have told him something. The silence of the sea birds wheeling overhead.

"Buy my pies," he sang out in practice, his boots cutting great gashes like exclamation marks in the sand.

Then he saw something washed up on the beach ahead.

Now fishermen often find things left along the shore. The sea gives and it takes and as often gives back again. There is sometimes a profit to be turned on the gifts of the sea. But every fisherman knows that when you have dealings with the deep you leave something of yourself behind.

It was no flotsam lying on the sand. It was a sea-queen, beached and gasping. John Merton stood over her, and his feet were as large as her head. Her body had a pale-greenish cast to it. The scales of her fishlike tail ran up past her waist, and some small scales lay along her sides, sprinkled like shiny gray-green freckles on the paler skin. Her breasts were as smooth and golden as shells. Her supple shoulders and arms looked almost boneless. The green-brown hair that flowed from her head was the color and texture of wrackweed. There was nothing lovely about her at all, he thought, though she exerted an alien fascination. She struggled for breath and, finding it, blew it out again in clusters of large, luminescent bubbles that made a sound as of waves against the shore.

And when John Merton bent down to look at her more

closely still, it was as if he had dived into her eyes. They were ocean eyes, blue-green, and with golden flecks in the iris like minnows darting about. He could not stop staring. She seemed to call to him with those eyes, a calling louder than any sound could be in the air. He thought he heard his name, and yet he knew that she could not have spoken it. And he could not ask the mermaid about it, for how could she tell him? All fishermen know that mermaids cannot speak. They have no tongues.

He bent down and picked her up and her tail wrapped around his waist, quick as an eel. He unwound it slowly, reluctantly, from his body and then, with a convulsive shudder, threw her from him back into the sea. She flipped her tail once, sang out in a low ululation, and was gone.

He thought, wished really, that that would be the end of it, though he could not stop shuddering. He fancied he could still feel the tail around him, coldly constricting. He went on to the fair, sold all his pies, drank up the profit and started for home.

He tried to convince himself that he had seen stranger things in the water. Worse—and better. Hadn't he one day brought up a shark with a man's hand in its stomach? A right hand with a ring on the third finger, a ring of tourmaline and gold that he now wore himself, vanity getting the better of superstition. He could have given it to his wife, Mair, but he kept it for himself, forgetting that the sea would have its due. And hadn't he one night seen the stars reflecting their cold brilliance on the water as if the ocean itself stared up at him with a thousand eyes? Worse—and better. He reminded himself of his years cull-ing the tides that swept rotting boards and babies' shoes and kitchen cups to his feet. And the fish. And the eels. And the necklaces of teeth. Worse—and better.

By the time he arrived home he had convinced himself of nothing but the fact that the mermaid was the nastiest and yet most compelling thing he had yet seen in the ocean. Still, he said nothing of it to Mair, for though she was a fisherman's daughter and a fisherman's wife; since she had been deaf from birth no one had ever let her go out to sea. He did not want her to be frightened; as frightened as he was himself.

But Mair learned something of it, for that night when John Merton lay in bed with the great down quilt over him, he swam and cried and swam again in his sleep, keeping up stroke for stroke with the sea-queen. And he called out, "Cold, oh God, she's so cold," and pushed Mair away when she tried to wrap her arms around his waist for comfort. Oh, yes, she knew, even though she could not hear him, but what could she do? If he would not listen to her hands on his, there was no more help she could give.

So, John Merton went out the next day with only his wife's silent prayer picked out by her fingers along his back. He did not turn for a kiss.

And when he was out no more than half a mile, pulling strongly on the oars and ignoring the spray, the sea-queen leaped like a shot across his bow. He tried to look away, but he was not surprised. He tried not to see her webbed hand on the oarlock or the fingers as sure as wrackweed that gripped his wrist. But slowly, ever so slowly, he turned and stared at her, and the little golden fish in her eyes beckoned to him. Then he heard her speak, a great hollow of sound somewhere between a sigh and a song, that came from the grotto that was her mouth.

"I will come," he answered, now sure of her question, hearing in it all he had longed to hear from his wife. It was magic, to be sure, a compulsion, and he could not have denied it had he tried. He stood up, drew off his cap and tossed it onto the waves. Then he let the oars slip away and his life on land slip away and plunged into the water near the bobbing cap just a beat behind the mermaid's flashing tail.

A small wave swamped his boat. It half-sank, and the tide lugged it relentlessly back to the shore where it lay on the beach like a bloated whale.

When they found the boat, John Merton's mates thought him drowned. And they came to the house, their eyes tight with grief and their hands full of unsubtle mimings.

"He is gone," said their hands. "A husband to the sea." For they never spoke of death and the ocean in the same breath, but disguised it with words of celebration.

Mair thanked them with her fingers for the news they bore, but she was not sure that they told her the truth. Remembering her husband's night dreams, she was not sure at all. And as she was a solitary person by nature, she took her own counsel. Then she waited until sunrise and went down to the shore.

His boat was now hers by widow's right. Using a pair of borrowed oars, she wrestled it into the sea.

She had never been away from shore, and letting go of

the land was not an easy thing. Her eyes lingered on the beach and sought out familiar rocks, a twisted tree, the humps of other boats that marked the shore. But at last she tired of the landmarks that had become so unfamiliar and turned her sights to the sea.

Then, about half a mile out, where the sheltered bay gave way to the open sea, she saw something bobbing on the waves. A sodden blue knit cap. John Merton's marker.

"He sent it to me," Mair thought. And in her eagerness to have it, she almost loosed the oars. But she calmed herself and rowed to the cap, fishing it out with her hands. Then she shipped the oars and stood up. Tying a great strong rope around her waist, with one end knotted firmly through the oarlock—not a sailor's knot but a love knot, the kind that she might have plaited in her hair—Mair flung herself at the ocean.

Down and down and down she went, through the seven layers of the sea.

At first it was warm, with a cool light blue color hung with crystal teardrops. Little spotted fish, green and gold, were caught in each drop. And when she touched them, the bubbles burst and freed the fish, which darted off and out of sight.

The next layer was cooler, an aquamarine with a fine, falling rain of gold. In and out of these golden strings swam slower creatures of the deep: bulging squid, ribboned sea snakes, knobby five-fingered stars. And the strands of gold parted before her like a curtain of beads and she could peer down into the colder, darker layers below.

Down and down and down Mair went until she reached the ocean floor at last. And there was a path laid out, of finely colored sands edged round with shells, and statues made of bone. Anemones on their fleshy stalks waved at her as she passed, for her passage among them was marked with the swirlings of a strange new tide.

At last she came to a palace that was carved out of coral. The doors and windows were arched and open, and through them passed the creatures of the sea.

Mair walked into a single great hall. Ahead of her, on a small dais, was a divan made of coral, pink and gleaming. On this coral couch lay the sea-queen. Her tail and hair moved to the sway of the currents, but she was otherwise quite still. In the shadowed, filtered light of the hall, she seemed ageless and very beautiful.

Mair moved closer, little bubbles breaking from her mouth like fragments of unspoken words. Her movement set up countercurrents in the hall. And suddenly, around the edges of her sight, she saw another movement. Turning, she saw ranged around her an army of bones, the husbands of the sea. Not a shred or tatter of skin clothed them, yet every skeleton was an armature from which the bones hung, as surely connected as they had been on land. The skeletons bowed to her, one after another, but Mair could see that they moved not on their own reckoning, but danced to the tunes piped through them by the tides. And though on land they would have each looked different, without hair, without eyes, without the subtle coverings of flesh, they were all the same.

Mair covered her eyes with her hands for a moment,

then she looked up. On the couch, the mermaid was smiling down at her with her tongueless mouth. She waved a
supple arm at one whole wall of bone men and they moved
again in the aftermath of her greeting.

"Please," said Mair, "please give me back my man." She
spoke with her hands, the only pleadings she knew. And
the sea-queen seemed to understand, seemed to sense a
sisterhood between them and gave her back greetings with
fingers that swam as swiftly as any little fish.

Then Mair knew that the mermaid was telling her to
choose, choose one of the skeletons that had been men.
Only they all looked alike, with their sea-filled eye sockets
and their bony grins.

"I will try," she signed, and turned toward them.

Slowly she walked the line of bitter bones. The first had
yellow minnows fleeting though its hollow eyes. The second had a twining of green vines round its ribs. The third
laughed a school of red fish out its mouth. The fourth had
a pulsing anemone heart. And so on down the line she
went, thinking with quiet irony on the identity of flesh.

But as long as she looked, she could not tell John Merton from the rest. If he was there, he was only a hanging
of bones indistinguishable from the others.

She turned back to the divan to admit defeat, when a
flash of green and gold caught her eye. It was a colder color
than the rest—yet warmer, too. It was alien under the sea,
as alien as she, and she turned toward its moving light.

And then, on the third finger of one skeleton's hand,
she saw it—the tourmaline ring which her John had so
prized. Pushing through the water toward him, sending

dark eddies to the walls that set the skeletons writhing in response, she took up his skeletal hand. The fingers were brittle and stiff under hers.

Quickly she untied the rope at her waist and looped it around the bones. She pulled them across her back and the white remnants of his fingers tightened around her waist.

She tried to pull the ring from his hand, to leave something there for the sea. But the white knucklebones resisted. And though she feared it, Mair went hand over hand, hand over hand along the rope, and pulled them both out of the sea.

She never looked back. And yet if she had looked, would she have seen the sea replace her man layer by layer? First it stuck the tatters of flesh and blue-green rivulets of veins along the bones. Then it clothed muscle and sinew with a fine covering of skin. Then hair and nails and the decorations of line. By the time they had risen through the seven strata of sea, he looked like John Merton once again.

But she, who had worked so hard to save him, could not swim, and so it was John Merton himself who untied the rope and got them back to the boat. And it was John Merton himself who pulled them aboard and rowed them both to shore.

And a time later, when Mair Merton sat up in bed, ready at last to taste a bit of the broth he had cooked for her, she asked him in her own way what it was that had occurred.

"John Merton," she signed, touching his fine strong arms with their covering of tanned skin and fine golden hair. "Tell me . . ."

But he covered her hands with his, the hand that was still wearing the gold and tourmaline ring. He shook his head and the look in his eyes was enough. For she could suddenly see past the sea-green eyes to the sockets beneath, and she understood that although she had brought him, a part of him would be left in the sea forever, for the sea takes its due.

He opened his mouth to her then, and she saw it was hollow, as dark black as the deeps, and filled with the sound of waves.

"Never mind, John Merton," she signed on his hand, on his arms around her, into his hair. "The heart can speak, though the mouth be still. I will be loving you all the same."

And, of course, she did.

BECOME A
WARRIOR

Both the hunted and the hunter pray to God.

The moon hung like a bloody red ball over the silent battlefield. Only the shadows seemed to move. The men on the ground would never move again. And their women, sick with weeping, did not dare the field in the dark. It would be morning before they would come like crows to count their losses.

But on the edge of the field there was a sudden tiny movement, and it was no shadow. Something small was creeping to the muddy hem of the battleground. Something knelt there, face shining with grief. A child, a girl, the youngest daughter of the king who had died that evening surrounded by all his sons.

The girl looked across the dark field and, like her mother, like her sisters, like her aunts, did not dare put foot onto the bloody ground. But then she looked up at the moon and thought she saw her father's face there. Not the father who lay with his innards spilled out into contorted hands. Not the one who had braided firesticks in his beard and charged into battle screaming. She thought she saw the father who had always sung her to sleep against the night terrors. The one who sat up with her when Great Graxyx haunted her dreams.

"I will do for you, Father, as you did for me," she whispered to the moon. She prayed to the goddess for the strength to accomplish what she had just promised.

Then foot by slow foot, she crept onto the field, searching in the red moon's light for the father who had fallen. She made slits of her eyes so she would not see the full horror around her. She breathed through her mouth so that she would not smell all the deaths. She never once thought of the Great Graxyx who lived—so she truly believed—in the black cave of her dressing room. Or any of the hundred and six gibbering children Graxyx had sired. She crept across the landscape made into a horror by the enemy hordes. All the dead men looked alike. She found her father by his boots.

She made her way up from the boots, past the gaping wound that had taken him from her, to his face which looked peaceful and familiar enough, except for the staring eyes. He had never stared like that. Rather his eyes had always been slotted, against the hot sun of the gods, against the lies of men. She closed his lids with trembling fingers and put her head down on his chest, where the stillness of the heart told her what she already knew.

And then she began to sing to him.

She sang of life, not death, and the small gods of new things. Of bees in the hive and birds on the summer wind. She sang of foxes denning and bears shrugging off winter. She sang of fish in the sparkling rivers and the first green uncurlings of fern in spring. She did not mention dying, blood, or wounds, or the awful stench of death. Her father already knew this well and did not need to be recalled to it.

And when she was done with her song, it was as if his corpse gave a great sigh, one last breath, though of course he was dead already half the night and made no sound at all. But she heard what she needed to hear.

By then it was morning and the crows came. The human crows as well as the black birds, poking and prying and feeding on the dead.

So she turned and went home and everyone wondered why she did not weep. But she had left her tears out on the battlefield.

She was seven years old.

Dogs bark, but the caravan goes on.

Before the men who had killed her father and who had killed her brothers could come to take all the women away to serve them, she had her maid cut her black hair as short as a boy's. The maid was a trembling sort, and the hair cut was ragged. But it would do.

She waited until the maid had turned around and leaned down to put away the shears. Then she put her arm around the woman, and with a quick knife's cut across her throat, killed her, before the woman could tell on her. It was a mercy, really, for she was old and ugly and would be used brutally by the soldiers before being slaughtered, probably in a slow and terrible manner. So her father had warned before he left for battle.

Then she went into the room of her youngest brother, dead in the field and lying by her father's right hand. In his great wooden chest she found a pair of trews that had probably been too small for him, but were nonetheless too long for her. With the still-bloody knife she sheared the legs of the trews a hand's width, rolled and sewed them with a quick seam. The women of her house could sew well, even when it had to be done quickly. Even when it had to be done through half-closed eyes. Even when the hem was wet with blood. Even then.

When she put on the trews, they fit, though she had to pull the drawstring around the waist quite tight and tie the rib bands twice around her. She shrugged into one of her brother's shirts as well, tucking it down into the waistband. Then she slipped her bloody knife into the shirt sleeve. She wore her own riding boots—which could not be told from a boy's—for her brother's boots were many times too big for her.

Then she went out through the window her brother always used when he set out to court one of the young and pretty maids. She had watched him often enough though he had never known she was there, hiding beside the bed, a dark little figure as still as the night.

Climbing down the vine, hand over hand, was no great trouble either. She had done it before, following after him. Really, what a man and a maid did together was most interesting, if a bit odd. And certainly noisier than it needed to be.

She reached the ground in moments, crossed the garden, climbed over the outside wall by using a tree as her ladder. When she dropped to the ground, she twisted her ankle a bit, but she made not the slightest whimper. She was a boy now. And she knew they did not cry.

In the west, a cone of dark dust was rising up and advancing on the fortress, blotting out the sky. She knew it for the storm that many hooves make as horses race across the plains. The earth trembled beneath her feet. Behind her, in their rooms, the women had begun to wail. The sound was thin, like a gold filament thrust in to her breast. She plugged her ears that their cries could not recall her to her old life, for such was not her plan.

Circling around the stone skirting of the fortress, in the shadow so no one could see her, she started around toward the east. It was not a direction she knew. All she knew was that it was away from the horses of the enemy.

Once, she glanced back at the fortress that had been the only home she had ever known. Her mother, her sisters, the other women stood on the battlements looking toward the west and the storm of riders. She could hear their wailing, could see the movement of their arms as they beat upon their breasts. She did not know if that was a plea or an invitation.

She did not turn to look again.

To become a warrior, forget the past.

Three years she worked as a serving lad in a fortress not unlike her own but many days' travel away. She learned to clean and to carry, she learned to work after a night of little sleep. Her arms and legs grew strong. Three years she worked as the cook's boy. She learned to prepare geese and rabbit and bear for the pot, and learned which parts were salty, which sweet. She could tell good mushrooms from bad and which greens might make the toughest meat palatable.

And then she knew she could no longer disguise the fact that she was a girl, for her body had begun to change in ways that would give her away. So she left the fortress, start-ing east once more, taking only her knife and a long loop of rope, which she wound around her waist seven times.

She was many days hungry, many days cold, but she did not turn back. Fear is a great incentive.

She taught herself to throw the knife and hit what she aimed at. Hunger is a great teacher.

She climbed trees when she found them in order to sleep safe at night. The rope made such passages easier.

She was so long by herself, she almost forgot how to speak. But she never forgot how to sing. In her dreams she sang to her father on the battlefield. Her songs made him live again. Awake she knew the truth was otherwise. He was dead. The worms had taken him. His spirit was with the goddess, drinking milk from her great pap, milk that tasted like honey wine.

She did not dream of her mother or of her sisters or of any of the women in her father's fortress. If they died, it had been with little honor. If they still lived, it was with less.

So she came at last to a huge forest with oaks thick as a goddess's waist. Over all was a green canopy of leaves that scarcely let in the sun. Here were many streams, rivulets that ran cold and clear, torrents that crashed against rocks, and pools that were full of silver trout whose meat was sweet. She taught herself to fish and to swim, and it would be hard to say which gave her the greater pleasure. Here, too, were nests of birds, and that meant eggs. Ferns curled and then opened, and she knew how to steam them using a basket made of willow strips and start a fire from rubbing sticks against one another. She followed bees to their hives, squirrels to their hidden nuts, ducks to their watered beds.

She grew strong, and brown, and—though she did not know it—very beautiful.

Beauty is a danger, to women as well as to men. To warriors, most of all. It steers them away from the path of killing. It softens the soul.

When you are in a tree, be a tree.

She was three years alone in the forest and grew to trust the sky, the earth, the river, the trees, the way she trusted her knife. They did not lie to her. They did not kill wantonly. They gave her shelter, food, courage. She did not remember her father except as some sort of warrior god, with staring eyes, looking as she had seen him last. She did not remember her mother or sisters or aunts at all.

It had been so long since she had spoken to anyone, it was as if she could not speak at all. She knew words: they were in her head, but not in her mouth, on her tongue, in her throat. Instead she made the sounds she heard every day—the grunt of boar, the whistle of duck, the trilling of thrush, the settled cooing of the wood pigeon on its nest.

If anyone had asked her if she was content, she would have nodded.

Content.

Not happy. Not satisfied. Not done with her life's work.

Content.

And then one early evening a new sound entered her domain. A drumming on the ground, from many miles away. A strange halloing, thin, insistent, whining. The voices of some new animal, packed like wolves, singing out together.

She trembled. She did not know why. She did not remember why. But to be safe from the thing that made her tremble, she climbed a tree, the great oak that was in the very center of her world.

She used the rope ladder she had made, and pulled the ladder up after. Then she shrank back against the trunk of the tree to wait. She tried to be the brown of the bark, the green of the leaves, and in this she almost succeeded.

It was in the first soft moments of dark, with the woods outlined in muzzy black, that the pack ran yapping, howling, belling into the clearing around the oak.

In that instant she remembered dogs.

There were twenty of them, some large, lanky grays; some stumpy browns with long muzzles; some stiff-legged spotted with pushed-in noses; some thick-coated; some smooth. Her father, the god of war, had had such a motley pack. He had hunted boar and stag and hare with such. They had found him bear and fox and wolf with ease.

Still, she did not know why the dog pack was here, circling her tree. Their jaws were raised so that she could see their iron teeth, could hear the tolling of her death with their long tongues.

She used the single word she could remember. She said it with great authority, with trembling.

"Avaunt!"

At the sound of her voice, the animals all sat down on their haunches to stare up at her, their own tongues silenced. Except for one, a rat terrier, small and springy and unable to be still. He raced back up the path toward the west like some small spy going to report to his master.

Love comes like a thief, stealing the heart's gold away.

It was in the deeper dark that the dogs' master came, with his men behind him, their horses' hooves thrumming the forest paths. They trampled the grass, the foxglove's pink bells and the purple florets of self-heal, the wine-colored burdock flowers and the sprays of yellow golden-rod equally under the horses' heavy feet. The woods were wounded by their passage. The grass did not spring back nor the flowers raise up again.

She heard them and began trembling anew as they thrashed their way across her green haven and into the very heart of the wood.

Ahead of them raced the little terrier, his tail flagging them on, 'til he led them right to the circle of dogs waiting patiently beneath her tree.

"Look, my lord, they have found something," said one man.

"Odd they should be so quiet," said another.

But the one they called lord dismounted, waded through the sea of dogs, and stood at the very foot of the oak, his feet crunching on the fallen acorns. He stared up, and up, and up through the green leaves and at first saw nothing but brown and green.

One of the large gray dogs stood, walked over to his side, raised its great muzzle to the tree, and howled.

The sound made her shiver anew.

"See, my lord, see—high up. There is a trembling in the foliage," one of the men cried.

"You fool," the lord cried, "that is no trembling of leaves. It is a girl. She is dressed all in brown and green. See how she makes the very tree shimmer." Though how he could see her so well in the dark, she was never to understand.

"Come down, child, we will not harm you."

She did not come down. Not then. Not until the morning fully revealed her. And then, if she was to eat, if she was to relieve herself, she had to come down. So she did, dropping the rope ladder, and skinning down it quickly. She kept her knife tucked up in her waist, out where they could see it and be afraid.

They did not touch her but watched her every movement, like a pack of dogs. When she went to the river to drink, they watched. When she ate the bit of journeycake the lord offered her, they watched. And even when she relieved herself, the lord watched. He would let no one else look then, which she knew honored her, though she did not care.

And when after several days he thought he had tamed her, the lord took her on his horse before him and rode with her back to the far west where he lived. By then he loved her, and knew that she loved him in return, though she had yet to speak a word to him.

"But then, what have words to do with love?" he whispered to her as they rode.

He guessed by her carriage, by the way her eyes met his, that she was a princess of some sort, only badly used. He loved her for the past which she could not speak of, for her courage which showed in her face, and for her beauty. He would have loved her for much less, having found her in the tree, for she was something out of a story, out of a prophecy, out of a dream.

"I loved you at once," he whispered. "When I knew you from the tree."

She did not answer. Love was not yet in her vocabulary. But she did not say the one word she could speak: *avaunt*. She did not want him to go.

*When the cat wants to eat her kittens, she says
they look like mice.*

His father was not so quick to love her.

His mother, thankfully, was long dead.

She knew his father at once, by the way his eyes were slotted against the hot sun of the gods, against the lies of men. She knew him to be a king if only by that.

And when she recognized her mother and her sisters in his retinue, she knew who it was she faced. They did not know her, of course. She was no longer seven but nearly seventeen. Her life had browned her, bronzed her, made her into such steel as they had never known. She could have told them but she had only contempt for their lives. As they had contempt now for her, thinking her some drudge run off to the forest, some sinister throwling from a forgotten clan.

When the king gave his grudging permission for their marriage, when the prince's advisers set down in long scrolls what she should and should not have, she only smiled at them. It was a tree's smile, giving away not a bit of the bark.

She waited until the night of her wedding to the prince when they were couched together, the servants a-giggle outside their door. She waited until he had covered her face with kisses, when he had touched her in secret places that made her tremble, when he had brought blood between her legs. She waited until he had done all the things she had once watched her brother do to the maids, and she cried out with pleasure as she had heard them do. She waited until he laid asleep, smiling happily in his dreams, because she did love him in her warrior way.

Then she took her knife and slit his throat, efficiently and without cruelty, as she would a deer for her dinner.

"Your father killed my father," she whispered, soft as a love token in his ear as the knife carved a smile on his neck.

She stripped the bed of its bloody offering and handed it to the servants who thought it the effusions of the night. Then she walked down the hall to her father-in-law's room.

He was bedded with her mother, riding her like one old wave atop another.

"Here!" he cried as he realized someone was in the room. "You!" he said when he realized who it was.

Her mother looked at her with half opened eyes and, for the first time, saw who she really was, for she had her father's face, fierce and determined.

"No!" her mother cried. "Avaunt!" But it was a cry that was ten years late.

She killed the king with as much ease as she had killed his son, but she let the knife linger longer to give him a great deal of pain. Then she sliced off one of his ears and put it gently in her mother's hand.

In all this she had said not one word. But wearing the blood of the king on her gown, she walked out of the palace and back to the woods, though she was many days getting there.

No one tried to stop her, for no one saw her. She was a flower in the meadow, a rock by the roadside, a reed by the river, a tree in the forest.

And a warrior's mother by the spring of the year.

AN INFESTATION
OF ANGELS

The angels came again today, filthy things, dropping golden-hard wing feathers and turds as big and brown as camel dung. This time one of them took Isak, clamping him from behind with massive talons. We could hear him screaming long after the covey was out of sight. His blood stained the doorpost where they took him. We left it there, part warning, part desperate memorial, with the dropped feathers nailed above. In a time of plagues, this infestation of angels was the worst.

We did not want to stay in the land of the Gipts, but slaves must do as their masters command. And though we were not slaves in the traditional sense, only hirelings, we had signed contracts and the Gipts are great believers in contracts. It was a saying of theirs that "One who goes back on his signed word is no better than a thief." What they do to thieves is considered grotesque even in this godforsaken desert-land.

So we were trapped here, under skies that rained frogs, amid sparse fields that bred locusts, beneath a sun that raised rashes and blisters on our sensitive skins. It was a year of unnature. Yet if anyone of us complained, the leader of the Gipts, the faró, waved the contract high over his head, causing his followers to break into that high ululation they mis-call laughter.

We stayed.

Minutes after Isak was taken, his daughter Miriamne came to my house with the Rod of Leaders. I carved my own sign below Isak's and then spoke the solemn oath in our ancient tongue to Miriamne and the nine others who came to witness the passing of the stick. My sign was a snake, for my clan is Serpent. It had been exactly twelve rotations since the last member of Serpent had led the People here, but if the plague of angels lasted much longer, there would be no one else of my tribe to carry on in this place. We were not a warrior clan and I was the last. We had always been a small clan, and poor, ground under the heels of the more prosperous tribes.

When the oath was done and properly attested to—we are a people of parchment and ink—we sat down at the table together to break bread.

"We cannot stay longer," began Josu. His big, bearded face was so crisscrossed with scars it looked like a map, and the southern hemisphere was moving angrily. "We must ask the faró to let us out of our contract."

"In all the years of our dealings with the Gipts," I pointed out, "there has never been a broken contract. My father and yours, Josu, would turn in their graves knowing we even consider such a thing." My father, comfortably dead these fifteen years back in the Homeland, would not have bothered turning, no matter what the cause. But Josu's father, like all those of Scorpion, had been the anxious type, always looking for extra trouble. It took little imagination to picture him rotating in the earth like a lamb on a holiday spit.

Miriamne wept silently in the corner, but her brothers pounded the table with fists as broad as hammers.

"He *must* let us go!" Ur shouted.

"Or at least," his younger, larger brother added sensibly, "he must let us put off the work on his temple until the angels migrate north. It is almost summer."

Miriamne was weeping aloud now, though whether for Isak's sudden bloody death or at the thought of his killers in the lush high valleys of the north was difficult to say.

"It will do us no good to ask the faró to let us go," I said. "For if we do, he will use us as the Gipts always use thieves, and that is not a happy prospect." By *us*, of course, I meant me, for the faró's wrath would be visited upon the asker, which, as leader, would be me. "But . . ." I paused, pauses being the coin of Serpent's wisdom.

They looked expectant.

"If we could persuade the faró that this plague was meant for the Gipts and not us . . ." I left that thought in front of them. The Serpent clan is known for its deviousness and wit, and deviousness and wit were what was needed now, in this time of troubles.

Miriamne stopped weeping. She walked around the

table and stood behind me, putting her hands on my shoulders.

"I stand behind Masha," she said.

"And I." It was Ur, who always followed his sister's lead.

And so, one by one by one, the rest of the minon agreed. What the ten agreed to, the rest of the People in the land of the Gipts would do without question. In this loyalty lay our strength.

I went at once to the great palace of the faró, for if I waited much longer he would not understand the urgency of my mission. The Gipts are a fat race with little memory, which is why they have others build them large reminders. The deserts around are littered with their monuments—stone and bone and mortar tokens cemented with the People's blood. Ordinarily we do not complain of this. After all, we are the only ones who can satisfactorily plan and construct these mammoth memories. The Gipts are incapable on their own. Instead they squat upon their vast store of treasures, doling out golden tokens for work. It is a strange understanding we have, but no stranger than some of nature's other associations. Does not the sharp-beaked plover feed upon the crocodile's back? Does not the tiny remora cling to the shark?

But this year the conditions in the Gipt kingdom had been intolerable. While we often lose a few of the People to the heat, to the badly-prepared Giptanese food, or to the ever-surprising visit of the Gipt pox, there had never before been such a year: plague after plague after plague. There were dark murmurs everywhere that our God had somehow been angered. And the last, this hideous infestation.

Normally angels stay within their mountain fasts, feasting on wild goats and occasional nestlings. They are rarely seen, except from afar on their spiraling mating flights when the males circle the heavens, caroling and displaying their stiffened pinions and erections to their females who watch from the heights. (There are, of course, stories of Gipt women who, inflamed by the Sight of that strange, winged masculinity, run off into the wilds and are never seen again. Women of the People would never do such a thing.)

However, this year there had been a severe drought and the mountain foliage was sparse. Many goats died of starvation. The angels, hungry for red meat, had found our veins carried the same sweet nectar. Working out on the monuments walking along the streets unprotected, we were easier prey than the horned goats. And the Gipts allow us to carry no weapons. It is in the contract.

Fifty-seven had fallen to the angel claws, ten of them of my own precious clan. It was too many. We had to convince the faró that this plague was his problem and not ours. It would take all of the deviousness and wit of a true Serpent. I thought quickly as I walked down the great wide street, the Street of Memories, towards the palace of the faró.

Because the Gipts think a woman's face and ankle can cause unnecessary desire, both had to be suitably draped. I wore the traditional black robe and pants that covered my legs, and the black silk mask that hid all but my eyes. However, a builder needs to be able to move easily, and it was hot in this land, so my stomach and arms were bare. Those parts of the body were considered undistinguished by the Gipts. It occurred to me as I walked that my stomach and arms were thereby flashing unmistakable signals to any angels on the prowl. My grip on the Rod of Leadership tightened. I shifted to carry it between both hands. I would not go meekly, as Isak had, clamped from behind. I twirled and looked around, then glanced up and scanned the skies.

There was nothing there but the clear, untrammeled blue of the Gipt summer canopy. Not even a bird wrote in lazy script across that slate.

And so I got to the palace without incident. The streets had been as bare as the sky. Normally the streets would be a-squall with the People and other hirelings of the Gipts. *They* only traveled in donkey-drawn chairs and at night, when their overweight, ill-proportioned bodies can stand the heat. And since the angels are a diurnal race, bedding down in their aeries at night, Gipts and angels rarely meet.

I knocked at the palace door. The guards, mercenaries hired from across the great water, their blackfaces mapped with ritual scars, opened the doors from within. I nodded slightly. In the ranks of the Gipts, the People were higher than they. However, it says in our holy books that all shall be equal, so I nodded.

They did not return my greetings. Their own religion counted mercenaries as dead men until they came back home. The dead do not worry about the niceties of conversation.

"Masha-la, Masha-la," came a twittering cry.

I looked up and saw the faró's twenty sons bearing down on me, their foreshortened legs churning along the hall. Still too young to have gained the enormous weight that marked their elders, the boys climbed upon me like little monkeys. I was a great favorite at court, using my Serpent's wit to construct wonder tales for their entertainment.

"Masha-la, tell us a story."

I held out the Rod and they fell back, astonished to see it in my hand. It put an end to our casual story sessions. "I must see your father, the great faró," I said.

They raced back down the hall, chittering and smacking their lips as the smell of the food in the dining commons drew them in. I followed, knowing that the adult Gipts would be there as well, partaking of one of their day-long feasts.

Two more black mercenaries opened the doors for me. Of a different tribe, these were tall and thin, the scarifications on their arms like jeweled bracelets of black beads. I nodded to them in passing. Their faces reflected nothing back.

The hall was full of feeding Gipts, served by their slimmer women. On the next-to-highest tier, there was a line of couches on which lay seven huge men, the faró's advisors. And on the high platform, overseeing them all, the mass of flesh that was the faró himself, one fat hand reaching toward a bowl of peeled grapes.

"Greetings, oh high and mighty faró," I said, my voice rising above the sounds in the hall.

The faró smiled blandly and waved a lethargic hand. The rings on his fingers bit deeply into the engorged flesh. It is a joke amongst the People that one can tell the age of a Gipt as one does a tree, by counting the rings. Once put on, the rings become embedded by the encroaching fat. The many gems on the faró's hand winked at me. He was very old.

"Masha-la," he spoke languidly, "it grieves me to see you with the Rod of your people."

"It grieves me even more, mighty faró, to greet you with my news. But it is something which you must know." I projected my voice so that even the women in the kitchens could hear.

"Say on," said the faró.

"These death-bearing angels are not so much a plague upon the People but are rather using us as an appetizer for Giptanese flesh," I said. "Soon they will tire of our poor, ribby meat and gorge themselves on yours. Unless . . ." I paused.

"Unless what, *Leader of the People*?" asked the faró.

I was in trouble. Still, I had to go on. There was no turning back, and this the faró knew. "Unless my people take a small vacation across the great sea, returning when the angels are gone. We will bring more of the People and the monument will be done on time."

The faró's greedy eyes glittered. "For no more than the promised amount?"

"It is for your own good," I whined. The faró expects petitioners to whine. It is in the contract under "Deportment Rules."

"I do not believe you, Masha-la," said the faró. "But you tell a good story. Come back tomorrow."

That saved my own skin, but it did not help the rest. "These angels *will* be after the sons of the faró," I said. It was a guess. Only the sons and occasional and unnecessary women still went out in the daylight. I am not sure why I said it. "And once they have tasted Gipt flesh . . ." I paused.

There was a sudden and very real silence in the room. It was clear I had overstepped myself. It was clearer when the faró sat up. Slowly that mammoth body was raised with the help of two of the black guards. When he was seated upright, he put on his helm of office, with the decorated flaps that draped against his ears. He held out his hand and the guard on the right pushed the Great Gipt Crook into his pudgy palm.

"You and your People will not go to the sea this year before time," intoned the faró. "But tomorrow *you* will come to the kitchen and serve up your hand for my soup."

He banged the crook's wide bottom on the floor three times. The guard took the crook from his hand. Then exhausted by the sentence he had passed on my hand—I hoped they would take the left, not the right—he lay down again and started to eat.

I walked out, through doors opened by the shadow men, whose faces I forgot as soon as I saw them, out into the early eve, made blood red by the setting sun. I could

hear the patter of the faró's sons after me, but such was my
agitation that I did not turn to warn them back. Instead I
walked down the street composing a psalm to the cun-
ning of my right hand, just in case.

The chittering of the boys behind me increased and,
just as I came to the door of Isak's house, I turned and
felt the weight of wind from above. I looked up and saw
an angel swooping down on me, wings fast to its side in a
perilous stoop like a hawk upon its prey. I fell back against
the doorpost, reaching my right hand up in supplication.
My fingers scraped against the nailed-up feathers. Instinctively I grabbed them and held them clenched in my fist.
My left hand was down behind me scrabbling in the dirt.
It mashed something on the ground. And then the angel
was on me and my left hand joined the right pushing up
against the awful thing.

Angel claws were inches from my neck when something stopped the creature's rush. Its wings whipped out
and slowed its descent, and its great golden-haired head
moved from side to side.

It was then that I noticed its eyes. They were as blue as
the Gipt sky—and as empty. The angel lifted its beautiful
blank face upward and sniffed the air, pausing curiously
several times at my outstretched hands. Then, pumping
its mighty wings twice, it lifted away from me, banked
sharply to the right, and took off in the direction of the
palace, where the faró's sons scattered before it like twigs
in the wind.

Two times the angel dropped down and came up with
a child in its claw. I leaped to my feet, smeared the top

of my stick with dung and feathers and chased after the beast, but I was too late. It was gone, a screaming boy in each talon, heading towards its aerie, where it would share its catch.

What could I tell the faró that he would not already know from the hysterical children ahead of me? I walked back to my own house, carrying my stick above my head. It would protect me as no totem had before. I knew now what only dead men had known, the learning which they had gathered as the claws carried them above the earth! *Angels are blind and hunt by smell.* If we but smeared our sticks with their dung and feathers and carried this above our heads, we would be safe; we would be, in their "eyes," angels.

I washed my hands carefully, called the minon to me, and told them of my plan. We would go this night, as a people, to the faró. We would tell him that his people were cursed by our God now. The angels would come for them, but not for us. He would have to let us go.

It was the children's story that convinced him, as mine could not. Luck had it that the two boys taken were his eldest. Or perhaps not luck. As they were older, they were fatter—and slower. The angel came upon them first.

Their flesh must have been sweet. In the morning we could hear the hover of angel wings outside, like a vast buzzing. Some of the People wanted to sneak away by night.

"No," I commanded, holding up the Rod of Leadership, somewhat darkened by the angel dung smeared over the top. "If we sneak away like thieves in the night, we will never work for the Gipts again. We must go tomorrow morning, in the light of day, through the cloud of angels. That way the faró and his people will know our power and the power of our God."

"But," said Josu, "how can we be sure your plan will work? It is a devious one at best. I am not sure even I believe you."

"Watch!" I said and I opened the door, holding the Rod over my head. I hoped that what I believed to be so was so, but my heart felt like a marble in the mouth.

The door slammed behind me and I knew faces pressed against the curtains of each window.

And then I was alone in the courtyard, armed with but a stick and a prayer.

The moment I walked outside, the hover of angels became agitated. They spiraled up and, like a line of enormous insects, winged toward me. As they approached, I prayed and put the stick above my head.

The angels formed a great circle high over my head and one by one they dipped down, sniffed around the top of the Rod, then flew back to place. When they were satisfied, they wheeled off, flying in a phalanx, towards the farthest hills.

At that, the doors of the houses opened, and the People emerged. Josu was first, his own stick, messy with angel dung, in hand.

"Now, quick," I said, "before the faró can see what we

are doing, grab up what dung and feathers you find from that circle and smear it quickly on the doorposts of the houses. Later, when we are sure no one is watching, we can scrape it onto totems to carry with us to the sea."

And so it was done. The very next morning, with much blowing of horns and beating of drums, we left for the sea. But none of the faró's people or his mercenaries came to see us off, though they followed us later.

But that is another story altogether, and not a pretty tale at all.

NAMES

Her mother's number had been 0248960. It was still imprinted on her arm, burned into the flesh, a permanent journal entry. Rachel had heard the stories, recited over and over in the deadly monotone her mother took on to tell of the camp. Usually her mother had a beautiful voice, low, musical. Men admired it. Yet not a month went by that something was not said or read or heard that reminded her, and she began reciting the names, last names, in order, in a sepulchral accent:

ABRAHMS
BERLINER
BRODSKY
DANNENBERG
FISCHER
FRANK
GLASSHEIM

GOLDBLATT

It was her one party trick, that recitation. But Rachel always knew that when the roll call was done, her mother would start the death-camp stories. Whether the audience wanted to hear them or not, she would surround them with their own guilt and besiege them with the tales:

HEGELMAN
ISAACS
KAPLAN
KOHN

Her mother had been a child in the camp; had gone through puberty there; had left with her life. Had been lucky. The roll call was of the dead ones, the unlucky ones. The children in the camp had each been imprinted with a portion of the names, a living yahrzeit, little speaking candles; their eyes burning, their flesh burning, wax in the hands of the adults who had told them: "You must remember. If you do not remember, we never lived. If you do not remember, we never died." And so they remembered.

Rachel wondered if, all over the world, there were survivors, men and women who, like her mother, could recite those names:

LEVITZ
MAMOROWITZ
MORGENSTERN

NORENBERG
ORENSTEIN
REESE

Some nights she dreamed of them: hundreds of old children, wizened toddlers, marching toward her, their arms over their heads to show the glowing numbers, reciting names.

ROSENBLUM
ROSENWASSER
SOLOMON
STEIN

It was an epic poem, those names, a ballad in alphabetics. Rachel could have recited them along with her mother, but her mouth never moved. It was an incantation. Hear, O Israel, Germany, America. The names had an awful power over her, and even in her dreams she could not speak them aloud. The stories of the camps, of the choosing of victims—left line to the ovens right to another day of deadening life—did not frighten her. She could move away from the group that listened to her mother's tales. There was no magic in the words that told of mutilations, of children's brains against the Nazi walls. She could choose to listen or not listen; such recitations did not paralyze her. But the names:

TANNENBAUM
TEITLEMAN

VANNENBERG
WASSERMAN
WECHTENSTEIN
ZEISS

Rachel knew that the names had been spoken at the moment of her birth: that her mother, legs spread, the waves of Rachel's passage rolling down her stomach, had breathed the names between spasms long before Rachel's own name had been pronounced. Rachel Rebecca Zuckerman. That final *Zeiss* had burst from her mother's lips as Rachel had slipped out greasy with birth blood. Rachel knew she had heard the names in the womb. They had opened the uterine neck, they had lured her out and beached her as easily as a fish. How often had her mother commented that Rachel had never cried as a child. Not once. Not even at birth when the doctor had slapped her. She knew, even if her mother did not, that she had been silenced by the incantation, the *Zeiss* a stopper in her mouth.

When Rachel was a child, she had learned the names as another child would a nursery rhyme. The rhythm of the passing syllables was as water in her mouth, no more than nonsense words. But at five, beginning to understand the power of the names, she could say them no more. For the saying was not enough. It did not satisfy her mother's needs. Rachel knew that there was something more she needed to do to make her mother smile.

At thirteen, on her birthday, she began menstruating, and her mother watched her get dressed. "So plump. So *zaftik*." It was an observation, less personal than a weather report. But she knew it meant that her mother had finally seen her as more than an extension, more than a child still red and white from its passage into the light.

It seemed that, all at once, she knew what to do. Her mother's duty had been the Word. Rachel's was to be the Word Made Flesh.

She stopped eating.

The first month, fifteen pounds poured off her. Melted. Ran as easily as candle wax. She thought only of food. Bouillon. Lettuce. Carrots. Eggs. Her own private poem. What she missed most was chewing. In the camp they chewed on gristle and wood. It was one of her mother's best tales.

The second month her cheekbones emerged, sharp reminders of the skull. She watched the mirror and prayed. *Barukh arah adonai elohenu melekh ha-olam.* She would not say the words for bread or wine. Too many calories. Too many pounds. She cut a star out of yellow poster board and held it to her breast. The face in the mirror smiled back. She rushed to the bathroom and vomited away another few pounds. When she flushed the toilet, the sound was a hiss, as if gas were escaping into the room.

The third month she discovered laxatives, and the names on the containers became an addition to her litany: Metamucil, Agoral, Senokot. She could feel the chair impress itself on her bones. Bone on wood. If it hurt to sit, she would lie down.

She opened her eyes and saw the ceiling, spread above her like a sanitized sky. A voice pronounced her name. "Rachel, Rachel Zuckerman. Answer me."

But no words came out. She raised her right hand, a signal; she was weaker than she thought. Her mother's face, smiling, appeared. The room was full of cries. There was a chill in the air, damp, crowded. The smell of decay was sweet and beckoning. She closed her eyes and the familiar chant began, and Rachel added her voice to the rest. It grew stronger near the end:

ABRAHMS
BERLINER
BRODSKY
DANNENBERG
FISCHER
FRANK
GLASSHEIM
GOLDBLATT
HEGELMAN
ISAACS
KAPLAN
KOHN
LEVITZ
MAMOROWITZ
MORGENSTERN
NORENBERG
ORENSTEIN
REESE
ROSENBLUM
ROSENWASSER
SOLOMON
STEIN

NAMES

TANNENBAUM
TEITLEMAN
VANNENBERG
WASSERMAN
WECHTENSTEIN
ZEISS
ZUCKERMAN

They said the final name together and then, with a little sputter, like a *yahrzeit* candle at the end, she went out.

STORY NOTES AND POEMS

The Weaver of Tomorrow

This story was published in my first book of original fairy tales, *The Girl Who Cried Flowers*, that launched my career and landed me with the title (from *Newsweek Magazine*) of "America's Hans Christian Andersen." Between Andersen and Oscar Wilde, I had discovered a longing to create new fairy tales. These are stories that walk like and talk like old tales but are brand new. In other words—not from the folk, but from a specific author. Though often these stories go back into the folk culture—"The Little Mermaid," "Beauty and the Beast," "The Ugly Duckling," "Goldilocks and the Three Bears" are popular "folk tales," but each one began as an original story by a specific author and from there moved out into the world, becoming "folk tales."

The poem below was one I wrote in answer to my

friend/co-author David L. Harrison, who had written a poem about a wheel and posted it on his blog in 2020.

The Wheel Spins

I am the spinner
of the yarns
that keep you warm
each night.

I am the weaver
of the dreams,
that help your heart
take flight.

Hand off the wheel,
I slow the tale
the strand that pulled
you in.

I draw the pattern,
for the day
and then begin
to spin.

I knit your bones,
I fill the hole,
I start the stitch
that sews your soul.

The White Seal Maid

"The White Seal Maid," one of the many selchie stories and poems I have written over the years, was first published in my own fairy tale collection called *The Hundredth Dove and Other Stories*, 1977. Selchies are folk tale creatures from Scotland and the Scandinavian countries. They are seal folk, but when they come ashore, they shed their sea skins and dance upon the sand. Though they dance joyously, at those moments they are incredibly in peril from humans who fall in love with them, steal their shed skins, and force them into marriages of a sort. I guess I am as obsessed by selchie stories as the humans who supposedly steal their skins.

The poem that follows has been turned into a gorgeous song by Lui Collins. We have since written many songs together. Here is a link to Lui singing it: https://www.youtube.com/watch?v=KbfhOJyL8Is. We ended up in a band together: Three Ravens. My grandson said to his father, "Nana's in a band? What does she play?" And my son Adam, a musician himself, never missing a beat, answered, "The audience." The poem was first published in my collection *Neptune Rising* in 1982.

Ballad of the White Seal Maid

The fisherman sits alone on the land,
his hands are his craft, his boat in his art,
The fisherman sits alone on the land,
a rock, a rock in his heart.

The selchie maid swims alone in the bay,
her eyes are the seal's, her heart is the sea,
The selchie maid swims alone through the bay,
a white seal maid is she.

She comes to the shore and sheds her seal skin,
she dances on the sand and under the moon,
her hair falls in waves all down her white skin,
only the seals hear the tune.

The fisherman stands and takes up her skin,
staking his claim to a wife from the sea,
he raises his hand and holds up the skin,
Saying: "Now you must come home with me."

Weeping she goes and weeping she stays,
her hands are her craft, her babes are her art,
a year and a year and a year more she stays,
a rock, a rock in her heart.

But what is this hid in the fisherman's bag?
it smells of the ocean, it feels like the sea,
a bony-white seal skin closed up in the bag,

and never a tear more sheds she.

"Good-bye to the house and good-bye to the shore,
Good-bye to the babes that I never could claim.
But never a thought to the man left on shore,
For selchie's my nature and name."

She puts on the skin and dives back in the sea,
The fisherman's cry falls on water-deaf ears.
She swims in her seal skin far out to the sea.
The fisherman drowns in his tears.

The Snatchers

I was reading some Jewish history as I worked on a book about my father's family, especially his oldest brother, who had been sent to a Russian military academy because he had been such a scoundrel as a teen. And what I found out was that Jews were rarely sent to such places, which fed directly into the Russian army, because of three factors: The food would not be kosher. They would have to march and do maneuvers on the Sabbath. They would probably never get to return home. Ever. But the army never conscripted an only boy child, leaving a family without a son. Nor did they take anyone who was in some way maimed, incapable of holding and shooting a rifle, or with foot or leg problems that would preclude walking many miles a day.

The Jewish answer to this was twofold. First they adopted out all but one of their sons to son-less members of their community. And if there weren't enough son-less members, they would cut off the boy's finger, or toe, effectively maiming him enough so as not to be army material. The army's response to that were the Snatchers, bounty hunters (sometimes Jewish themselves) who snatched up the boys before either of these things could occur.

I was so surprised by this information, I knew I had to write the story. It was published by *F&SF Magazine* in 1993, and later was reprinted in the anthology *Masterpieces of Horror*.

The poem comes from a book of poems I wrote about my father's family in the Ukraine and their immigration to America, a memoir in verse called *Ekaterinoslav*, published in 2012. Lou was the bad boy sent to the military academy, and in the end sent across to America to anchor the family that would come a few years later, in two waves. My father, the second youngest, came in the last wave.

Lou Leaving Home

We do not know how easily he leaves,
escaping his father's wrath,
his mother's tears,
his sisters' casual relief,
the younger children's disbelief.
Does he turn and smile? Blow kisses?
Does he use the front of his hand, the back,
as if leaving takes no courage at all?

Or is he already far-seeing,
like a sailor well used to travel,
eyes squinting into the sun;
imagining the road to the big ship,
plotting the route across the waves,
dreaming of America's streets
shining in the sun like gold.
Surely, he'd already counted
the cards to be played,
having learned in his old school,
to gamble the Russian way:
no mercy given, none received.

Wilding

I wrote this story for an anthology, *Starfarer's Dozen*, 1995,
and it is driven by three things. The first is New York
City and the apartment house I grew up in on 97th and
Central Park West. Not only did I play in Central Park
with friends, take my younger brother Steve for walks and
games in the park, but I was transfixed by the large building next door, "The First Church of Christ, Scientist,"
though I never went in.

Second, I am fascinated by tales of creatures/humans
who can shift shapes, be they vampires, werewolves, su-
perheroes, or in this case those kids who go out "wilding."

Third, I am a huge fan of Maurice Sendak's picture
book *Where the Wild Things Are*, which had a lot of influ-

ence on this short story. The picture book begins with a boy—Max—who goes wilding in his wolf suit with actual Wild Things before sailing home to his supper, which is still hot.

However the actual term "wilding" had hit the news around the time I was working on the story (in the 1980s). It was used to label teens in gangs who ran through Central Park, beating up runners and raping young women. A group of young black teens were charged with savagely beating and raping one female runner so viciously she could not recall what had happened to her. Someone else eventually confessed to the deed, his confession was corroborated, and the boys were set free.

The poem below was written back in 2012, but this is its first publication.

Deer, Dances

The day, the night I was a deer,
little leaves and shoots tempted me,
acorns in their hard jackets,
and the wild white clover.
River became my only drink,
running over twenty-one stones.
I did not mind getting wet.
Doe my woman, sang to me,
and the little spotted fawn, my family,
cheered as I danced by,
the white flag of my tail
semaphoring my joy at speaking,

at dancing with my little brothers.
All the while, my hooves
struck turquoise from the rock,
leaving a jeweled trail.
You watched me run until the dawn,
sweat glistening on my hide,
the moon resting in my antlers.
I shall return to you soon,
but not so soon I have left
the flint of my soul behind.

Requiem Antarctica (with Robert J. Harris)

I had an idea. My novels usually start with an idea, my
short stories with a first line. The idea for this story was
simple but fascinating—that polar explorer Robert Falcon
Scott, bitten by a vampire when still in England, and finding himself now one of that horrid crew, takes on the task
of leading a crew of explorers to the Pole in the hopes to
cool his hot vampiric blood. When crewman Oates, upon
whom he had been feeding after his own blood supplies
and assorted birds and other creatures ran out, said, "I am
just going outside and may be some time" (this is a true
part of Scott's well-documented adventure), Scott knew
his own time was up and he hoped no one would ever find
his own body, a double sacrifice.

Okay—I had the idea, but that was all except for several bad tries at a beginning and no real plot to speak of.

I was in Scotland having dinner with my friends Debby and Bob Harris, and spilled the vampiric beans. (We three are all published writers and dinner conversations often are about things we are writing.) Bob—with whom I'd written several published short stories and eight published novels—said in his almost unparsable Dundonian accent that he was a huge Falcon Scott fanatic and had many rare books about the man. Bob is also a plot genius. "Let's write it together," I said. We did, and sold it very quickly to *Asimov's Science Fiction Magazine* in 2000. Frankly, I always thought it should be longer—novella length. But we never got around to writing that.

The poem first came out in the anthology *The Mammoth Book of Vampire Stories by Women* in 2001, edited by the indefatigable anthologist Stephen Jones, and then as lyrics for a song by the group *Folk Underground*.

Vampyr

We stalk the dark,
Live in the flood.
We take the madness
In the blood.

A moment's prick,
A minute's pain
And then we live
To love again.

Drink the night.

Rue the day.

We hear the beat
Beneath the breast.
We sip the wine
That fills the chest.

A moment's prick,
A minute's pain,
Our living is not
Just in vein.

> *Drink the night,*
> *Rue the day.*

We do not shrink
From blood's dark feast.
We take the man,
We leave the beast.

A moment's prick,
A minute's pain,
We live to love
To live again.

> *Drink the night,*
> *Rue the day.*

Night Wolves

Yes, I was one of those kids—who hear and see and smell things at night. Had nightmares. And middle child, son Adam, took after me. As an adult, he solved it by becoming super-dark in his own writing. Fighting fire with fire. In my adulthood, I stopped worrying about bears and wolves and started worrying about burglars and jewel thieves. (I don't have those kinds of jewels!) And then I got an alarm system. As I live in a small town, the police are very quick to get to me, as the station is only half a block away from my house. I found out how fast they responded when I pushed a button on a necklace I found in my bedside table. I hadn't remembered it was an alarm, the kind for old ladies who may fall in the middle of the night. Before I could figure out how to shut it off, there was a policeman at my door! *Nightwolves* was first published in an anthology called *The Haunted House* in 1995.

The poem was first published in a small magazine called *Silver Blade* in 2013.

Bad Dreams

They come like reivers
on hardy nightmare nags,
crossing the borders
between waking and sleep.
Early winter is best,

when nights are long.
I fear them greatly,
for they steal away my rest.
Last night you came to me
in your steel bonnet,
death's head staring straight out.
I knew you by your blue eyes,
those eyes that had followed me
for sleepless nights six years ago
when you died, your hand in mine.
I live in a Peel Tower now,
heart fortified against assault.
Love may try to smoke me out
but I will outwait and outwit you,
waking to a better morning.

The House of Seven Angels

I do not remember writing this story, or where I found out about all those angels. (I am 80, and the story was published in a collection of mine called *Here There Be Angels*, 1996, more than twenty years ago.) But several things I do know about the story: it is set in the same town as my grandfather Samson, grandmother Manya, and their eight children had lived. My father had been seven years old when they came to America, escaping the next pogrom.

The poem's first publication is in this book.

Anticipation

Water drop
on the lip of a spout.

Trout lifting itself
after a fly.

Villella suspended
in mid-leap.

The night before
Chanukah.

Everything depends
on the gravity of angels

and that long fall into day.

Great Gray

So much about this story is true: the setting, the crazy
lady, the irruption of Great Gray owls in Hatfield, the little town I have lived in for the past 50 years. My husband,
a passionate birder, taught us all to bird. Our youngest
son, Jason, at the time this story is set, was ten years old,
rode his bike all around town showing itinerant birders

where to the find the owls. Also, I came upon a bizarre group of people who seemed to be worshiping in a small swampy grove near the outskirts of town, kneeling down one after another as if in prayer. They turned out to be kneeling at the foot of the tree where a Great Gray eyed them in a puzzled manner, as they took his picture with their cameras. (This was long before cell phones existed!)

Jason is now approaching fifty, with a wife and twin teenage daughters, so no one murdered him as a child. A bit of poetic license. He's a professional photographer and writer, taking photographs of nature—birds and fish mainly. Has won awards for his photography and has more than 25 books out, illustrated with his photographs. This story was first published in an anthology called *Fires of the Past* in 1991.

This poem was written for this book and first published here.

Remembering the Great Gray

I remember the winter of our Great Grays
three of them down from the Canadian wilds,
scavenging for moles, voles, mice under the turf.
They were as welcome as the busloads of birders
who drove up from Pennsylvania to genuflect
under a dead tree where a cloud in bird shape,
a specter with feathers, mesmerized them all
with its marbled yellow eyes.

My husband fed the owls white mice from a pet store,

our ten-year-old son became a tour guide on a bike.
We could not go a day without a bird report.
They were down by the dike. Two flew across River Road.
I watched one eat a weasel, swallowed it whole.

If we could have grown feathers, rain-cloud colored,
we would have flown north with them,
back to the taiga, wind puzzling through our wings.
But Nature, ever a cynic, dismisses such magic,
for she has her own.

Little Red (with Adam Stemple)

An invitation to an anthology, and I began to write a Little
Red Riding Hood variant. It began to go too dark for me
and I (quite literally) lost the plot. So I called upon my
Prince of Darkness, aka The Plot God—my son Adam
Stemple, with whom I have written many stories and
books. (He always ups the body counts in our books.)
He made the story darker, and bloodier, but in the best
possible way, and I cleaned up what little there was with
my cap, like a good Red Cap soldier should. I am only
making a little bit of this up. It's mostly true. The rest is
metaphor. The anthology was *Firebirds Soaring*, edited by
Sharyn November, published in 2009.

This poem is first published in this book.

JANE YOLEN

Red at Eighty-One

So you thought to fool me again,
you old bastard, with your sweet growls,
your shoulders broad enough
to carry in the wood without sweat,
your big eyes blinking out lies,
your promises of cakes and wine.
You think you can cozen me,
undress me, steal my nightgown,
my skin, my bones, take me in,
devour me whole, leave me nothing
of myself, not even a shadow,
not even a memory.
You believe I have learned nothing
in seventy-four years, that the woods
have taught me little: the scurrying ants
carrying ten times their own weight,
dung beetles rolling their foul burdens,
coyotes wallowing in rotting meat,
vultures, with their appetites
worn around naked necks.
You are wrong, old man, mistaking me
for an innocent, counting on my curiosity,
expecting my obedience, requiring my silence.
I am too old for such nonsense.
I'll eat you up this time.

Winter's King

There was a wonderful artist (alas, name forgotten) who did a fantasy painting of a sere and stunning "Winter's King." The painting got picked up as cover art for Martin Greenberg's fantasy anthology that was a bow to Tolkien's work, *After the King*, published in 1991. Marty and I had edited a bunch of books together, so he asked me to write an introduction and a story for the book. This was my story. I didn't mean it to go where it did, but the story had set its mind on a quasi-tragedy and didn't let me know until the end.

This poem's first publication is in this book.

If Winter

If winter has a king,
then surely Frost is his fool,
speaking a kind of frozen truth
to the powers of wind and snow.
He takes a little nip at the nose
of his bottle of schnapps
and hurries into a soliloquy
about ice and its uses,
about the power of cold,
before light-footed Spring comes in
and sits on Old King Winter's lap
persuading him with soft breaths
to hand over the kingdom
for another useless half a year.

Inscription

My husband and I bought a house in St Andrews, Scotland, which we'd been renting during his second sabbatical. He was a professor of computer science at the University of Massachusetts in Amherst, and already working with people at St. Andrews University. It became our summer home. I still go there every summer to write and to see dear friends I have made over the more than 30 years there.

We did a lot of driving around and investigating Scottish sites, sometimes just the two of us, or with visitors (and occasionally our grown children). Sometimes I accompanied him on computer science conferences in interesting places. At one of the latter, we discovered a grand circle of stones. And the first two lines of this story sprang into my head. When we returned home, the rest followed. The story was first published in an anthology called *Ultimate Witch*, 1993, that I had just been invited into, and then appeared in *Year's Best Fantasy and Horror* anthology. I still have quite a fondness for the story.

This poem was written for this book.

<u>Stone Ring</u>

Touch the stone,
cold with the death
of the Pictish makers.

Cold with the nights
of the reivers' rivers,
crossed to steal some koos.

Colder than the dead
at grey Cullodon,
fighting for Charlie's greed.

History's reminders:
Ghosts in stone.
We die together or alone.

The ring binds us all.

Dog Boy Remembers

I wrote a few public posts back and forth on a folklore site called *Sur La Lune* as a kind of challenge/writing prompt with the wonderful writer Midori Snyder. It became a short story and then a novel, which we sold. One of the characters whom I liked especially was the compromised anti-hero Dog Boy. He was half-human, raised by his Red Cap father as a sort of pet, though he was human. (A Red Cap is a particularly nasty kind of murderous gremlin who dips his hat in the blood of his victims.) But Dog Boy is saved in the end by his love for a complicated young human woman and the memory of his human mother.

However, we never delved into his back story in the novel. Years later, being invited into a fantasy literary journal, *Unnatural Worlds, Fiction River #1*, published in 2013, I decided to write Dog Boy's birth story. As I knew, it was not going to be a sweet story.

The Path

Step onto the path,
let it wind and unwind
along the silver stream.
Here bluebells wave,
ferns uncurl,
puffballs reveal their heft,
and the paw print of a dog
who has gone ahead
shows you where to go.
You can smell the darkness
and the light,
taste it on the air.
Time compresses,
and then like the road,
unwinds into the rest of your life.
That is the only magic that counts.
The only magic.
It is in your hand, your mouth,
your heart, your belly.
It is on the road.

The Fisherman's Wife

Ah—mermaids. Not always Ariel. This one grew dark and darker.

I like strong women. Come from a family of them. So this moral and mortal battle between two strong women for the love of a drowning fisherman, was a no-brainer for me. Just a bit on the wet side. It became part of my collection *Neptune Rising*, 1982, a book of mermaid/merman stories and poems. The poem was first published there as well.

Undine

It is a sad tale,
the one they tell,
of Undine
the changeling,
Undine
who took on legs
to walk the land
and dance
on those ungainly stalks
before a prince
of the earthfolk.
He betrayed her;
they always do
the landsmen.
Her arms around him
meant little more

than a finger of foam
curled around his ankle.
Her lips on his
he thought cold,
brief and cold
as the touch of a wave.
He betrayed her,
they always do,
left her to find
her way back home
over thousands of land miles,
the only salt her tears,
and she as helpless
as a piece of featherweed
tossed broken onto the shore.

Become a Warrior

Sometimes a story starts in one direction and while the author stops thinking about it, it makes sharp turn. As this one did. On a quiet morning I was trying to write a story for a *Warrior Princesses* anthology a friend was putting together and published in 1982. The story—which I'd envisioned as a positive, uplifting story—went darker, and then darker still. Sometimes a story has its own mind and the author has to run after it shouting, "Wait for me. . . ."

As for the poem, it is published here for the first time.

The Princess Turns

Looking in the mirror,
the princess turns,
skirts bivalving around her.
    She looks little like a dragon,
though once her nails were hard,
brown, broken.
    Her hair once crinkled,
cracked, split-ended,
dyed green.
    Her belly once bloated,
bones bleached, eyes runny,
teeth yellowed.
    Amazing what a night
in a spa, good dentists,
detox, delousing can do.
    The princess turns.

An Infestation of Angels

For some odd reason, the first few paragraphs of this re-
boot of the Biblical Exodus came to me when I was on a
ten-day author tour (plus dogsledding trip) in Fairbanks,
Alaska, in March. It wasn't that I was dreaming of the
sun of the Middle East as an antidote to snow and frost.
Rather the young woman who'd been appointed my spirit

guide by the Arts Council that brought me there showed me an angel story she'd written (as I recall it was quite wonderful). It became a kind of challenge. Her angels were the golden kind. Mine are . . . NOT. I borrowed a typewriter from my host's home (quick—who knows what a typewriter is?) and got down the first paragraphs. Another possible point of interest—I minored in Comparative Religions at Smith College, along with majoring in English Lit, so I knew the Hebrew Testament quite well. The story was published in *Asimov's Magazine*, 1985.

This poem is first published in this book.

<u>Work Days</u>

There is work to do, angels,
roll up your gossamer sleeves.
Shutter your wings.
Leave the halo rusting
by the side of the road.
The world turns by labor,
not just hymns.

Pickers in the field know this.
Workers in the factory know this.
Artists at their easels know this.
Teachers in their classrooms know this.
Even the poet, in her moment
of inspiration grasps this knowledge.
Why is it so hard for others
to think this through?

News you do not like is still news.
So, do your work.

Names

In order to fill out a book of my fantasy short stories to be published by Peter Bedrick Books (a publisher known for its Jewish books, though this was not a collection of Jewish stories), I wrote this short Holocaust survivor tale. It has been reprinted a number of times and also may have been my first-ever story in *Year's Best Horror Fiction*. You never know how far a story will go to find its audience.

The poem was first published in my second political collection of poems, *Before/The Vote/After* in 2017. So now you know which way I lean. Left.

What the Oven Is Not

The oven is no sanctuary;
The food knows it, the Jew knows it.
Oil poured on, water bubbles out,
We crisp as easily as chicken,
though not as kosher.
Cancers, like stuffing, fill the gaps.
I'd not know, nor do I care
what you think of the Shoah.
I have spent half a lifetime

writing about it, intruding into the pain
my family—ever early adopters—
escaped via immigration and long luck.
There is a sickness here,
but it bears no name.
The oven knows it, and does not say.

AFTERWORD: FROM THE PRINCESS TO THE QUEEN

Alethea Kontis

Heidi E. Y. Stemple loves to tell the story of the year I showed up at Phoenix Farm for the Picture Book Boot Camp (PBBC) Master Class taught by her and her mother, Jane Yolen.

"I found out one of our students wore a tiara and fancied herself a princess—can you imagine? I couldn't wait to tell Mom. Of course, she immediately ran upstairs to fetch a crown. Because this girl might call herself a princess, but J. Y. is the *Queen*."

I'm a big fan of this recollection, so I never quibble, and I never get tired of hearing it. It's a great story, it's 100% true, and I like the way Heidi tells it.

But I remember my meeting with Jane a little differently.

Once upon a time, a girl named Truth wanted to attend the court of the Fairy Queen. Truth was a wild girl who'd become princess of a kingdom by the sea, but the coffers were bare, and so she did not have the money to go. But she was a clever girl. She managed to con a crafty leprechaun out of his gold (several leprechauns, if you must know) and made the long journey north.

Yes, my name really is the Greek word for Truth, and the day I signed onto LiveJournal as "PrincessAlethea," the entire science-fiction world picked up the nickname and ran with it. But Jane Yolen is so much more than a dread Fae Queen: she is a goddess. Jane Yolen does it all. Horror Writers Association, Science Fiction and Fantasy Writers of America (SFWA), Society of Children's Book Writers and Illustrators (SCBWI). Poetry, short stories, kids' books, song lyrics. Collections of magical tales full of snatchers and selkies, weavers and wolves, sunlight and starlight and everything in between. You name it, Jane Yolen has written it down on paper. She's been publishing longer than I've been alive, and I'm not that young.

To say I have idolized her my whole life would definitely be an understatement.

It started with three of us that spring in Massachusetts—all the best fairy tales start with threes. We flew in the night before PBBC started in earnest and had rooms reserved for us at the inn. Jane extended an invite to join her on her daily walk early the next morning (the Master Class didn't officially start until later that afternoon). The two older students declined, as they were best friends and had a lot of catching up to do, but the youngest student, full of energy and enthusiasm, took Jane up on the offer.

I'd read the fairy tales. I knew. When wise fairies ask you to walk with them through the woods, *you say yes.*

I even wore my tiara.

I was always going to be the cuckoo in that nest of students. The goal of every PBBC attendee was to utilize Jane's and Heidi's tutelage to raise their picture-book prowess to the next level. Every single one of us had published at least one picture book, but they all knew Jane exclusively through SCBWI. I was a chemistry major who'd been raised in the publishing industry, and at Dragon Con. *AlphaOops* might have been the first publishing contract I signed, but by the time it was released, I was a bona fide active member of SFWA.

My conversation with Jane during that first walk covered a little bit of everything: her time as an editor at Random House, her stint as president of SFWA, Shakespeare, shoes, ships, ceiling wax, the whole kit and caboodle. By the end of that walk, I had a true mentor, and Jane understood I wasn't the kind of princess who signed away her firstborn because she didn't take the time to read the fine print.

She knew (from one of my manuscript submissions) that my family had escaped from its own holocaust, during the Great Fire of Smyrna in 1922. A different dark wood, but a dark wood from which Jane had all too much experience telling difficult tales.

But I didn't tell her my whole story—that week, it was my job to hear far more stories than I told. She noted that I listened with the heart of a yarnspinner, that I saw with the eyes of a talesmith, that I dreamed with the mind of a weaver. She was familiar with the nightmares whence I came, although she did not know the exact paths I had walked to get to this place. I did not tell her in so many words that she was also my Baba Yaga, allowing me to seek refuge from a past where I had been abused by men. None of that mattered at Phoenix Farm. Baba Yolen challenged me until I was confident enough to triumph on my own.

But I think maybe, deep down, she knew all this anyway. Because sometimes kindred spirits and benevolent fairies know things without having to say a word.

It was never Jane's job to save me from anything—by the time we became friends, I had already saved myself. Nor was it her task to remind me how strong I am; once forged, it is impossible for a sword to forget it is a sword. But she reminded me in personal emails and poetry what it was to be real, to be Truth, both within fiction and without. She gave me tools so that I could better tell the hard tales. She encouraged me to investigate the wild wood that birthed me, so that I might discover animal friends in that darkness, or wings of my own, or even love. She taught me, by example, that the whirlwind inside my brain could be harnessed and even tamed, in time. She believed in me when I spread myself so thin that I forgot to believe in myself anymore.

She still believes in me. And takes great pride in telling me so, over and over and over again.

After that one morning's walk, Jane and I were destined to be friends forever, but it was the poem that sealed the deal. We were having lunch at the Eric Carle Museum a few days later on a Master Class field trip; there were giant posters across one wall of the cafeteria featuring the subjects of past exhibits.

"I would have loved to have seen the Quentin Blake one," I sighed. "His illustrated Ogden Nash book was one of my absolute favorites as a child. All my friends loved Shel Silverstein, but I always thought Ogden Nash was far more clever."

Jane turned and stared at me. *"If called by a panther . . ."*

"Don't anther," I finished.

That's right. Jane Yolen started a quote from an Ogden Nash poem, and I finished it. To the best of my knowledge, that sort of scene only happened in movies or television, when a teacher of great intelligence tests his or her student, and the student rises to the occasion. That thing that only played out in fiction had just played out in my actual life. With Jane Yolen.

We always dream of meeting our heroes, forging bonds and becoming the best of friends. I'm here to tell you that you're never really prepared for when that *actually happens.*

It was even scarier for me on some level because Jane wasn't just a colleague, mentor, and fairy godmother . . . she was *me.* It was as if I'd been handed a looking glass into the future. I was already a Princess Who Did Too Much, but here was the Queen of Everything, telling me there was no reason it couldn't be done. Because she'd gone and done it. All she had to do was point the way to the eighth square and send me on my way.

I always wished I'd met someone like Jane when I was a kid—it would have helped a lot to have known that being a Queen of Everything was a legitimate Life Path. This is why I most enjoy meeting middle schoolers—I can be for them the person I didn't have when I was twelve, a washed-up television actress in the middle of my first novel, with dozens of poems shoved in the shoebox under my bed.

But I have Jane now, better late than never. She is the goal. She is who I want to be when I never grow up. She is the reason I venture forth into this upside-down world, sad and strong and optimistic and constantly inspired, sword and head held high, unafraid because I know it is possible to do Everything. No bar has been invented that is too high for me to cross.

Except for maybe hers.

And I'm okay with that.

If Jane is the Queen and I'm the Princess, it should come as no surprise that she is Ringleader of this Midnight Circus, and I host my very own Traveling Sideshow.

Queen Jane traveled south to my kingdom once, the Chaos Realm of Dragon Con. The first thing we did (after breakfast, of course) was go for a walk. I gave her a tour. I marched behind her in a parade where they cheered for her from the streets. I escorted her to a formal dinner where the bard heckled me from the stage. I attended her reading. I brought her a crown.

I was asked to moderate the Young Adult Guest of Honor Panel that year: It was just Jane and me at the big table up on the dais, the Princess and the Queen.

"Can one of you test the microphones for me?" the sound tech yelled from the back.

I leaned forward. *"'Twas brillig and the slithy toves did gyre and gimble in the wabe . . ."*

"All mimsy was the borogoves, and the mome raths out-grabe," Jane finished into her own mic.

And so the universe maintains its balance.

Long Live Queen Jane!

Beloved fantasist Jane Yolen has been rightfully called the Hans Christian Andersen of America and the Aesop of the twentieth century. In 2018, she surpassed 365 publications, including adult, young adult, and children's fiction; graphic novels; nonfiction; fantasy; science fiction; poetry; short-story collections; anthologies; novels; novellas; and books about writing. Yolen is also a teacher of writing and a book reviewer. Her best-known books are *Owl Moon*, the How Do Dinosaurs series, *The Devil's Arithmetic, Briar Rose, Sister Emily's Lightship and Other Stories*, and *Sister Light, Sister Dark.*

Among Yolen's many awards and honors are the Caldecott and Christopher medals; the Nebula, Mythopoeic, World Fantasy, Golden Kite, and Jewish Book awards; the World Fantasy Association's Lifetime Achievement Award; the Science Fiction/Fantasy Writers of America

Grand Master Award; and the Science Fiction Poetry Grand Master Award. Six colleges and universities have given her honorary doctorates.

Yolen lives in Western Massachusetts and Mystic, Connecticut, with her fiancé, but spends long summers in St. Andrews, Scotland, a great place to write, she says, for there are nearly twenty hours of daylight and bird-song.

Theodora Goss is the World Fantasy and Locus Award–winning author of the short story and poetry collections *In the Forest of Forgetting* (2006), *Songs for Ophelia* (2014), and *Snow White Learns Witchcraft* (2019), as well as novella *The Thorn and the Blossom* (2012), debut novel *The Strange Case of the Alchemist's Daughter* (2017), and sequel *European Travel for the Monstrous Gentlewoman* (2018). The final novel in the series, *The Sinister Mystery of the Mesmerizing Girl*, was published in October 2019. She has been a finalist for the Nebula, Crawford, Seiun, and Mythopoeic Awards, as well as on the Tiptree Award Honor List. Her work has been translated into twelve languages. She teaches literature and writing at Boston University and in the Stonecoast MFA Program. Visit her at theodoragoss.com.

New York Times bestselling author Alethea Kontis is a princess, storm chaser, and geek. Author of more than 20 books and 40 short stories, Alethea is the recipient of the Jane Yolen Mid-List Author Grant, the Scribe Award, the Garden State Teen Book Award, and two-time winner of the Gelett Burgess Children's Book Award. She has been twice nominated for both the Andre Norton Nebula and the Dragon Award. When not writing or storm chasing, Alethea narrates stories for multiple award-winning online magazines, contributes regular YA book reviews to *NPR*, and hosts Princess Alethea's Traveling Sideshow every year at Dragon Con. Born in Vermont, she currently resides on the Space Coast of Florida with her teddy bear, Charlie. Find out more about Princess Alethea and her wonderful world at aletheakontis.com

Extended Copyright

All stories copyright © Jane Yolen unless otherwise noted.

"The Weaver of Tomorrow" copyright © 1974. First appeared in *The Girl Who Cried Flowers and Other Tales* (Crowell: New York).

"The White Seal Maid" copyright © 1977. First appeared in *The Hundredth Dove and Other Tales* (Crowell: New York).

"The Snatchers" copyright © 1993. First appeared in *The Magazine of Fantasy & Science Fiction*, October–November 1993.

"Wilding" copyright © 1995. First appeared in *A Starfarer's Dozen: Stories of Things to Come* (Jane Yolen/Harcourt: New York).

"Requiem Antarctica" copyright © 2000 by Jane Yolen and Robert J. Harris. First appeared in *Asimov's Science Fiction*, May 2000.

"Night Wolves" copyright © 1995. First appeared in *Haunted House: A Collection of Original Stories,* edited by Martin H. Greenberg and Jane Yolen (HarperCollins: New York).

"The House of the Seven Angels" copyright © 1996. First appeared in *Here There Be Angels* (Harcourt Brace: New York).

"Great Gray" copyright © 1991. First appeared in *Fires of the Past: Thirteen Contemporary Fantasies about Hometowns,* edited by Anne Devereaux Jordan (St. Martin's Press: New York).

"Little Red" copyright © 2009 by Jane Yolen and Adam Stemple. First appeared in *Firebirds Soaring: An Anthology of Original Speculative Fiction,* edited by Sharyn November (Firebird/Penguin: New York).

"Winter's King" copyright © 1991. First appeared in *After the King: Stories in Honor of J. R. R. Tolkien,* edited by Martin H.

Greenberg (Tor Books: New York).

"Inscription" copyright © 1993. First appeared in *The Ultimate Witch*, edited by John Gregory Betancourt and Byron Preiss (Byron Preiss Visual Publications: New York).

"Dog Boy Remembers" copyright © 2013. First appeared in *Fiction River Anthology: Unnatural Worlds*, edited by Kristine Kathryn Rusch and Dean Wesley Smith (WMG Publishing: Lincoln City, Oregon).

"The Fisherman's Wife" copyright © 1982. First appeared in *Neptune Rising: Songs and Tales of the Undersea People* (Philomel Books: New York).

"Become a Warrior" copyright © 1998. First appeared in *Warrior Princesses*, edited by Martin H. Greenberg and Elizabeth Ann Scarborough (DAW Books: New York).

"An Infestation of Angels" copyright © 1985. First appeared in *Asimov's Science Fiction Magazine,* November 1985.

"Names" copyright © 1983. First appeared in *Tales of Wonder* (Schocken Books: New York).

Poetry

"The Wheel Spins" copyright © 2020. First appeared in David L. Harrison's blogpost, "Wheel, Part 2," in comments. June 4, 2017.

"Ballad of the White Seal Maid" copyright © 1982. First appeared in *Neptune Rising: Songs and Tales of the Undersea People* (Philomel Books: New York).

"Lou Leaving Home" copyright © 2012. First appeared in *Ekaterinoslav: One Family's Passage to America: A Memoir in Verse* (Holy Cow! Press: Duluth, MN).

"Deer, Dances" copyright © 2020. First appearance.

"Vampyr" copyright © 2001. First appeared in *The Mammoth Book of Vampire Stories by Women*, edited by Stephen Jones (Carroll & Graf: New York).

"Bad Dreams" copyright © 2013. First appeared in *Silver Blade Magazine*.

"Anticipation" copyright © 2020. First appearance.

"Great Gray" copyright © 2020. First appearance.

"Red at Eighty-One" copyright © 2020. First appearance.

"If Winter" copyright © 2020. First appearance.

"Stone Ring" copyright © 2020. First appearance.

"The Path" copyright © 2020. First appearance.

"Undine" copyright © 1982. First appeared in *Neptune Rising: Songs and Tales of the Undersea People* (Philomel Books: New York).

"The Princess Turns" copyright © 2020. First appearance.

"Work Days" copyright © 2020. First appearance.

"What the Oven Is Not" copyright © 2017. First appeared in *Before/The Vote/After: A Book of Poems* (Levellers Press: Amherst, MA).